Sandbar Sisters

A SUMMER COTTAGE NOVEL

REBECCA REGNIER

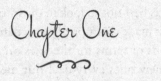

Chapter One

Libby

Elizabeth Quinn Malcolm stared at the small flatscreen TV in her kitchen. The monitor was tastefully hidden behind a panel in the backsplash, so it didn't clash with her solid surface quartz countertop. She'd painstakingly selected the countertop to achieve that modern farmhouse vibe.

The news reporter spoke in the present tense, as though this was happening right now, at six pm, on a Friday night. When in fact, it had actually happened over the last few months, right under Libby's nose.

"Prosecutors are working as we speak to decide whether to charge Elizabeth Quinn Malcolm for embezzlement. Malcolm is the founder and president of Southtown Now, a prominent community development company focused on renovating Southtown, Illinois neighborhoods."

Libby watched a video of herself fill the screen as the anchor continued. The clip was from last summer when she'd kicked off a 5K charity fundraiser.

She stared at her own face on the screen. Funny, the "elevens" that now looked like two canyons between her eyes were completely absent in the video. How was that only last summer? Libby didn't have the thousand bucks to drop on fillers these days. She decided it was best not to look in the mirror right now.

Elevens, who made that up? Elevens, parenthesis, crow's feet— here were millions of terms for the lines on a woman's face. They were inventing new ones every day! But men were rugged. Libby wasn't allowed to look rugged. No woman was.

What she saw in the file video, though, was a woman at the top of her game. Running the charity 5K and actually *running* in it. She was so confident! She was giving her all for her community and lowering cholesterol at the same time!

Libby never did one thing at a time. Always two, but more likely five.

Now Libby stood still, paralyzed. Multi-tasking was out of reach. She could barely even uni-task as her life unraveled.

The woman that stood in the kitchen now was also burning calories. But they were the worst kind, the calories that panic, fear, and gut awful realizations sizzle away from your body. It felt like a corrosive poison had seeped into her body. It eroded her strength, her confidence, her purpose.

The news anchor continued to explain the alleged crimes of Elizabeth Quinn Malcolm to the greater Chicago area news viewer.

"Forensic accountants discovered over five hundred thousand dollars missing from the non-profit. The question now is, where is it? And did a woman who claimed to be raising money for the community really steal it for herself? We'll continue to follow the story and bring you the latest as it develops."

Libby knew where it was; in a manner of speaking, anyway. Her husband of twenty-six years had siphoned it away. Dribs and drabs at first, to cover his gambling, to cover his lifestyle, to cover his tracks. Dribs and drabs that turned into an ocean.

Libby had discovered it too late. Henry had taken a midlife

crisis, packed it with dynamite, and blew up their lives. She didn't think it was malicious or targeted at her specifically. Henry didn't want to hurt her. He was in the middle of a gambling addiction. But the effect was the same, whether he meant to hurt her or not.

Her career was in ruins, along with her reputation, her marriage was broken, and she very well could be charged with embezzlement.

She'd done nothing wrong. She'd built Southtown Now from the ground up. She'd secured donations, lured prestigious board members, and they'd gotten real work done. Her entire sense of self was tied up in pride that this forgotten historic neighborhood was a better place now because of her.

But now, because of her, her management of the non-profit looked incompetent at best, dirty at worst.

Libby had a call to make. It was time. Her biggest donor with the deepest pockets, Reginald Bellamy hadn't pulled out of Southtown Now yet. God love him.

Reggie was her friend, maybe her only one right now. He had sent her a message of support. She thought that would be enough, but it wasn't.

Libby had to fall on her sword, or her association with Henry would drag down her life's work. Reggie's support was the one bright spot, but she needed to do the right thing.

She dialed the number, his private cell. A number many asked her for, but one she never shared. She knew it was a privilege to have access to Reginald Bellamy, owner of We Go Fuel Centers all over the state.

"How are you doing, Libby?" Reggie's deep voice on the other end had always been a comfort to her. He deployed his voice with conviction when he when issuing orders to his staff, but with kindness when helping her learn the ropes of big time corporate giving.

"Did you see the news?"

"Yes, I did. You know I'm behind you."

3

"I know, thank you. I'm stepping down, effective immediately."

"You can fight it, you know. Let them prove it all in court."

"I know, but that distracts from our work, what we've built. I step down, and you can find a new director. Distance yourself from Henry. From me."

"There wouldn't be a Southtown Now if it wasn't for you. This is a tough one."

"Nah, easy call. I'm out. Do you want me to write a news release for you to issue?"

"Could you?"

"Yep." Libby knew Reggie didn't love details like that. Libby had endeared herself to him more than once by dealing with details.

"Libby, thank you."

Reggie was a friend; she'd been right about that. "It's okay. Southtown Now has a fighting chance without my current predicament weighing it down."

"I owe you one for falling on your sword here. Don't forget, I pay up. Call if you need anything."

"Thanks, Reggie."

Reginald Bellamy was a self-made man. He had interests all over the Chicago area. He didn't owe her one, but it was nice that he said it.

"You'll land on your feet, kid. I know it."

Libby ended the call.

She felt shaky, strange. Next to her kids, her work had defined her life. And now poof! Gone! Just like her marriage. Just like her ability to trust the Brazilian hardwood floor on which she walked.

Poof. Gone.

Libby's life was in jagged pieces, but the solid surface countertops sure did look nice. They could, in fact, survive knives, heat, and total domestic annihilation, just like the sales brochure claimed.

Libby clicked off the television. She looked around her kitchen. It used to be filled with her kids, their friends, her husband, the couples they'd palled around with, and their lives. It was empty now.

The kids were grown. All three were in various stages of figuring out their own lives. They were good kids. They checked in with her when this all blew up. But she'd warned them to stay away. No need for them to be hounded by the news. Or to be guilty by association with Henry or her.

On impulse, Libby grabbed the decorative sign on her countertop. She was possessed by the urge to act out, to do damage to something.

She walked out to their three-car garage, sign in hand, and scanned the wall. The tools were meticulously placed in case the man-of-the-house needed to fix something.

Then she saw what she wanted. A hammer!

She slammed down the sign she'd snatched off her kitchen counter onto the center of the tool bench. She realized the bench was as decorative as the sign. Henry had never fixed a thing in his life. Just the books.

She took the hammer and raised it above her head with both hands. She brought it down solidly on the sign. The wood split in two. She did it again. The splintering of the wood was easily accomplished, no match for her frustration. Libby hit it again, for good measure.

There.

She put the hammer down gently, next to the destroyed sign. She took a breath. It caught in her throat. She inhaled again and exhaled. Libby reached up and ran her fingers through her hair. She patted the little moisture at her neck.

Okay.

She had lawyers to call.

The sign had read: *Live, Laugh, Love*. Libby was one for three on that triumvirate right now. She was technically alive, but it wasn't funny, and love? She was fresh out.

"It should say livid, loser, larceny," she mumbled to herself. *Where was the decorative sign for that?*

She left the sign in pieces.

Chapter Two

Emma

Sometimes her hand shocked her. It was her mother's, right? It couldn't possibly be hers. Those veins were so blue, the skin was thin as tissue. She massaged her knuckles.

Then there were those dark spots. Who knew about sunscreen in the forties?

She sat at the desk at the back of the house. Every corner of the house was designed to take advantage of the lake view. The home was massive, but her brilliant father had planned every inch.

The writing desk was in the corner, but the lake view was everywhere. The little peninsula that jutted into the lake ensured that it felt like you were on a ship when you looked out any window. It was almost as if you were floating on the water.

She loved that about the house.

The first paper she had to sign was easy, her will. This was going to make a few people very angry. Though they shouldn't be surprised. Emma had no children. She had nieces, nephews, great nieces, and ingrate nephews. Her will was a fluid thing. They should have known that. She never promised anyone. They all assumed. She chuckled at the thought.

The second paper sealed the deal. Nothing about this one made her chuckle. This little stroke of the pen on the deed would bring the Irish Hills back to life or consign it to the dustbin.

Take that!

"Phht!" It wasn't a word; it was a sound, but it conveyed all she needed it to.

Emma never sounded more like her Irish grandmother than when she was disgusted.

She stood up slowly, placing her knuckles on the desk for relief and support. She walked toward the back of the house.

The windows needed washing, or maybe replacing. The management of this home was always a job. She'd been a good steward of it, she believed, for most of her life. But she was tired now. This house needed to be in hands strong enough to scrub when needed or point straight when required. Emma couldn't confidently pronounce, "You missed a spot" because her eyes were missing many of the spots these days. Though, surely, a spot *was* missed—they always missed a spot.

These musings reaffirmed what she'd just done.

The lake was gray right now. It matched the sky. She looked west. This was the biggest lake in Lenawee County, Lake Manitou. The name was a shortened version of the word *michemanetue*, Lake of the Evil Spirit. The name had no connection to the peace and beauty here. Emma's heaven looked like Lake Manitou.

The lake was older than she was. So was the house, which was saying something these days.

Emma had devoted many years in her nine decades to learning about this land and these waters. She knew that many of the names of the places were a mishmash. Indian Agent Henry Schoolcraft had named counties and lakes by combining indigenous words he'd learned from his wife with Latin and Arabic. Just like Mississippi was a French rendering of an Ojibwe word, Manitou was an American rendering of a Potawatomi word.

Schoolcraft's wife was called Woman of the Sound that the Stars Make Rushing Through the Sky. Now that was a name!

Emma Ford Libby's name may not live much longer, but this place was going to live on. This place was going to be preserved, and so was this town.

A cool breeze whistled through the windows. Ice gripped Lake Manitou. All seasons were beautiful to her eyes, all days a miracle at this late stage of her life, even this icy one.

But summer was on the way. That was when the lake was in its full glory.

In the summer, from Memorial Day to Labor Day, Emma believed there was no better place on this earth. Years ago, this town and its vitality reflected that. They escaped the heat of Chicago, Detroit, and Toledo in Irish Hills. Before air conditioning or airplanes, this was the way to holiday. Her father knew this.

Was.

The word 'was' popped up a lot in her mind. Past tense.

Irish Hills, Michigan, had seen better days. The town had been a wreck since that awful day. But it didn't have to be that way.

This lake and the fifty others within a twenty-mile radius of the old main street were gold mines. People were noticing now.

And that was the issue. An issue she'd decided to take firmly in her blue-veined hands.

One more paper to sign.

The last paper was a letter. Brief, to the point, but adamant.

Given what was happening to her niece, Emma knew there wasn't much of a choice. She was to be the life raft for Libby Quinn Malcolm.

Even if Libby didn't know it.

Emma walked back to the writing desk. She signed her name in bold, sure strokes. Emma Ford Libby, the 'e,' the 'f,' the 'l' written in big, florid cursive.

The wheels were in motion.

Chapter Three

Libby

Dear Elizabeth,

I am leaving you Nora House. I realize this is a shock and might be somewhat out of the blue. Mainly since I am still alive, though older than dirt.

I hope you look upon your summers in Irish Hills with fondness. I certainly do.

The house is yours. Of my friends and family, you are the one who I believe can bring it back to life. It is yours to take now. My only condition is that you get here soon. I'm older than I can even remember. Tick tock.

I await your arrival. I know you've been through some trying times of late.

I have always found the lake house to be a balm for whatever ails me.

Regards,
   Your Aunt
   Emma Ford Libby

P.S. I do know that a secret kept you from returning. Don't let a secret from the past ruin your future one day longer.

   P.P.S., I know you prefer people address you as Libby, but that's our SURNAME, not a first name. Your mother could not be persuaded. I promise to try to call you Libby when you arrive.

Libby kept the old Jeep. That was it. The contents of her house, her curated objects, even her throw pillows were a part of the sale. Everything must go. And it did.

It was how she paid for the lawyer who'd argued, successfully, that Libby hadn't swindled Southtown Now.

Thank goodness for that.

Libby wasn't a felon, woo hoo! Amazing what she considered an accomplishment these days. She couldn't exactly brag on Facebook about that.

While her old friends posted adorable grandchildren photos or effusive love for their husbands, Libby could only brag that she didn't get charged with a Class One Felony.

Fan-frigging-tastic.

Henry was charged, but of course, he'd skipped town when this all went to heck.

Henry, her ex. She needed to start referring to Henry as an ex. That was another check she'd written to the lawyer: divorce proceedings on a spouse who'd fled the country. Normally, twelve months is required to constitute abandonment, officially. Her lawyer got it down to six. Thank goodness for her lawyer.

Libby sat in the driver's seat of her Jeep, packed with everything she now owned. She'd donated all but one of her power suits to charity. Someone at Goodwill was going to hit the jackpot of designer stilettos. She didn't mourn the loss of pretty shoes, not one bit.

Honestly, they hurt like hell.

And she'd been bruised in ways she didn't expect over this last year.

Libby sat in the driveway and looked up at the house for a moment.

The house was so beautiful. She'd made it so. Her real estate agent raved how much the buyers loved the décor. It was Pinterest come to life.

All that she'd built with Henry had slipped through her fingers. Someone else would build a life here, now.

That reminded her.

Libby yanked her wedding rings off her left hand. She shoved them in her purse. Maybe the rings would be a deposit on an apartment or surprise repair to the Jeep.

Libby looked at the manicured hedge that hugged the front of the house. She'd kept it all together, just so.

The Jeep, they'd bought it for the kids. It was ten years old, and she was grateful now to have it free and clear. No payments or loan. Their leased vehicles were turned in months ago. It was just Libby, the Jeep Wrangler, and some stuff. She'd kept only the "does it bring you joy" stuff. Marie Kondo would be so proud.

She'd been brutal as she assessed the accumulated stuff of their lives. Good dishes to goldfish bowls. Everything must go.

Family pictures, a ceramic vase her son made, a knitted baby blanket and her good flip flops made the cut. But not much else.

All of the joy "stuff" that survived her purge and sale fit neatly in the Jeep.

She did wish the Jeep wasn't red. Libby wasn't feeling red these days. Even when it came to her auburn hair. Libby looked in her rearview mirror and flattened her hair along her part.

She'd never gone this long without touching up her roots.

Who had the energy for that? Much less the expense. She could fill the Jeep's gas tank five times for what they charged at her old salon!

Libby loved her hair color and had done a lot to maintain it. Her own mother thought Libby's hair was a 'throwback.' Her mother said it with disdain. She said it to indicate someone somewhere on her dad's side. Whatever, that was ancient history. Still, her red hair used to make her feel rebellious. Back when she had the energy for that sort of thing.

Libby considered getting a box of hair color, but she was wise enough to know dying your own hair during a personal crisis were the actions of the truly deranged. She may be down, but she wasn't completely unglued.

She'd have to keep the roots a while longer.

Libby had one suitcase of clothes, and a box with a few pieces of more bits of jewelry. It was the only thing she had as insurance if things got worse.

Worse? She hoped not.

Libby was ready. She looked at the dashboard. Nearly eighty thousand miles on this thing. By the time she got to the lake, there'd be another three hundred on the dial.

The GPS on her phone said it would take about four hours to get to Irish Hills.

The letter from Aunt Emma was in her bag, on the seat next to her.

The idea that she would move to the lake, a place she hadn't been in thirty years, would have sounded insane only a few months ago.

Libby had thought if she avoided prosecution, she'd be in the clear. But not being charged isn't the same as clear.

No one in the greater Chicago area wanted to hire the community development organizer they'd seen on the news. She hadn't swindled anyone. But it had been her face next to the headlines.

After her legal troubles ended, Libby had assumed she'd easily find a new job. Yet from the network of business contacts she'd curated, as carefully as she'd curated those throw pillows, one door after another closed. That provided another reality check. Libby was damaged goods and unemployable in her chosen field.

She had nowhere to live and no job.

Her kids were worried. She hated that. She'd worked hard to be sure they didn't have to worry, and now she was the worry.

Libby had lied to them when they asked if they could help. No. No, they couldn't. This was her mess. She'd figure out the next part of her life. She had to.

"I'm fine. I'm all set. Don't be silly."

She had no idea what this next part looked like. Or what she wanted. It was an unfamiliar place to be.

Type A. That's what they called her when they were being nice.

Control freak. That's what they called her when they were sick of her planning or pushing.

She'd had zero control for the last few months. It was all a spiral, sucking her down, trying to drown her. Libby felt like she'd been hanging on by her formerly gel manicured nails for a long time. Too long.

Then she got the letter.

Aunt Emma and Lake Manitou.

It was a stop gap. A place to rest. She'd loved the lake so much when she was a girl.

She'd go there.

Aunt Emma had to be in her nineties now. The woman was probably batty. Libby had no doubt the offer to leave her the house was ridiculous. Probably the carrot Aunt Emma had dangled in front of everyone she knew to get her way.

And the P.S. the comment about secrets? Well, she did have a secret. Did Emma know it? Or was her aunt making a guess? Libby's secrets at the lake could be where she'd hid beer when they were fifteen or those skimpy bathing suits she and her friends bought behind their mothers' backs. Libby brushed aside the cryptic P.S. and focused on the practical. She needed a place to crash!

Her aunt was offering her a place to land and lick her wounds.

It didn't have to be more than that. Right now, the lake was the only place she could think of where her face wasn't synonymous with failure, or worse, embezzlement. And it was within her budget: free.

She'd regroup at the old lake house, Nora House, named after Libby's great grandmother, in Irish Hills, Michigan. This was the temporary plan until she figured out what was next.

She backed out of the driveway of her life.

Everything must go.

* * *

It was particularly warm for late April. That was a good sign, Libby decided. She needed good signs.

She pushed open the sunroof of the Jeep and let the smell of lilacs waft in as she sat at the exit. She'd skirted Lake Michigan out of Chicago and had taken 94 East through Indiana. She was in Michigan now, past Jackson. She was almost there.

Three small highways came together outside of Irish Hills. At US 223, Libby branched off. She'd need to turn left on Manitou Lake Road. That would take her straight into Irish Hills. She relied on her GPS, but it all started to feel familiar. Her father had driven them this way many times in her youth. Libby recognized the lake air, if not the turn-by-turn directions.

She was close. Water, sand, and mossy grass mixed together to let her know this was the place.

The smell in the air took her back to 1989 faster than hearing Fine Young Cannibals on her radio.

Her best summer days were spent here with some of the best friends she'd ever had.

Had.

And she hadn't been back, what, in thirty years?

Irish Hills, Michigan, was the smallest of small towns.

But it was a hub. There were fifty lakes within a twenty-five-mile radius of the one-stoplight town's main drag. Summers here were about boating, fishing, floating, tubing, skiing, kayaking, and just loafing. She'd done all of it during those summers.

They were called kettle lakes, depressions left behind from the glaciers that covered this part of the country eleven thousand or so years ago. Many of the lakes were named after places in Ireland. Places her own ancestors probably remembered fondly.

Except for Lake Manitou.

That was different. Libby didn't know as much as she should about the area but that she did remember.

Lake Manitou was the largest, the Grand Daddy.

The family lake house, Nora House sat atop a hill, facing west and presiding over the fifteen-hundred-acre lake.

Libby was named after her grandmother, on her father's side, except in reverse. Alice Libby Quinn was her grandmother. She was Elizabeth Alice Quinn Malcolm.

Once upon a time, the Libby family did business with Henry Ford. That's where most of the family legends and family money were born. Both the legends and the money had dissipated over the decades. And all Libby had left were fuzzy old stories from her childhood and that name.

The stories of her grandmother might be faded. But there was nothing pale about her memories of summers here. They were dayglo orange, hot pink, electric blue, and as she drove into town, they became more vivid.

What was it about that time in life that stayed? More so than anything that happened in her twenties or thirties. She could remember her favorite bathing suit, her favorite ice cream order at Tut's Place, the complete lyrics to 'We Didn't Start the Fire,' and how the boy who pumped gas at the marina looked in a cut-off t-shirt. But a password she created yesterday? Nope!

She grew up a little more every summer here. Until she'd grown up too much.

Libby pulled into downtown Irish Hills. She drove slowly down Manitou Lake Road and tried to take in the view.

She saw that Tut's Place was now boarded up, abandoned. Two scoops of bubblegum flavor in a sugar cone. That was her order.

Charming brick store fronts lined the main drag of Manitou Lake Road, but not-so-charming boards covered up most of the windows.

Gap-toothed. That described downtown Irish Hills these days.

Buildings, a church roof, and even a school had been destroyed the last summer she was here, and, by the looks of things, most had never been rebuilt.

The ghost town vibe added a layer of sadness on top of her already melancholy mood.

The town was a pale shadow of the adorable small tourist town that she remembered. Maybe this visit was a mistake. What was that Thomas Wolfe quote, "You can't go home again"?

Libby reminded herself this wasn't home; this was always a vacation spot. Irish Hills was always her Brigadoon. It was a magical once-a-year place filled with sun and friends and boys.

It was never her real life.

How boy crazy they all were back then. It made her laugh even now.

Well, now she wasn't here to date or to shop or buy souvenirs. She was here to lick her wounds without having to pay rent.

That was the grown-up truth.

The GPS instructed her to drive through town, straight at the one-stoplight at Lake Manitou and Green Street, continue on four blocks, and go south at Round Lake Highway. Round Lake was a road and a lake as well. It circled Manitou and Round. The two were connected by a small channel, but they were separate lakes. She'd water-skied both.

Was water skiing like riding a bike? Probably not.

She turned off her GPS. She decided to test her memory and find the old lake house without her smartphone ordering her around.

Left on Round Lake. That had to be correct. She knew that. She could see the lake over the trees in spots. It was a sunny afternoon and darn it if it didn't sparkle.

Wow, it was beautiful.

Flashes of burgers on a grill, laying on the raft, and the Sandbar Sisters all played in rapid-fire in her mind.

She passed small roads that shot off Round and towards the water. She read the street signs out loud, street names she'd forgotten for decades. Each small lane led to the lake. They were all dotted with cottages. The little streets ended at the water's edge with the best cottages sitting right on the beach. Clearwater, Holly Hock, Bullhead Point, Cedar Point, these were the landmarks of her youth. The places she'd pedaled around on her ten-speed bike with no hands.

Libby leaned forward over the steering wheel. She turned down the radio.

It had to be up next.

There it was, Sandy Beach Lane. There was a sign, but Libby was relieved to know she didn't need it. Her memory hadn't failed her. She knew where to go.

Sandy Beach Lane was a gravel road lined with trees. It wasn't as lush as it would get later in the season. The buds were just starting to open, the little flowers were almost wary of the winter air that lurked after sunset. It could still snow here in April. The cold could still freeze the fragile buds. But the trees wouldn't die, even if those buds took a beating. They knew how to survive.

The overgrown branches made Sandy Beach Lane feel a little like driving through a tunnel. The branches scraped the top of the Jeep and snapped back from the windshield as Libby drove down the old road.

Where is it?

Libby had her eye out for the small cottage, the only other one on this lane. It was the guest cottage, and sometimes she and her friends had crashed there.

It was there, still. Exactly where Libby expected it to be. She felt relief that her memory was accurate. The windows were boarded; roof shingles were missing. It was a shame it was so neglected. You would think this would be a perfect weekend getaway, something people on Airbnb would love.

Wow. If Libby had been feeling young for a moment, the guest cottage cured it. Every day of the last thirty years was etched on the shingles like it felt etched on her face right now.

She wondered how long it had been like this. And for a moment, it scared her.

Was the main lake house going to be in a similar state?

Nora House was a grand lady. Or Libby remembered it to be that way. She was worried now. Maybe she was driving to a haunted house, not the lake house of her memory.

She continued to drive the gravel lane. She emerged from the tree cover and into the clearing. But the home wasn't what filled her vision first.

Lake Manitou took her breath away. It stretched out as far as she could see on the horizon.

The Jeep slowed to a crawl as she maneuvered to a parking place next to the house. Even if the house had fallen into disrepair, this spot was worth a million dollars, in Libby's estimation. It was a little peninsula that provided water views on three sides and privacy that many homes on the lake, didn't have.

The lake house.

Libby tore her gaze from the water to the house. To her relief, it didn't disappoint. The massive Shingle Style mansion was as she remembered. Beautiful.

She'd seen examples of homes like this on the East Coast, but very few in the Midwest. It was a throwback to the days when her great grandfather walked in lock step with auto barons. People remembered Henry Ford, but Ford was part of a whole generation of men who made their fortunes on four wheels.

The shingles were painted white, though it looked like a new paint job was in order. The side facing the drive was lovely, but it only hinted at the porch that started on the side and wrapped around to the back.

The back of the lake house faced the lake. That was where anyone with eyes would want to be. She knew that inside almost every room was a lake view.

Libby turned off the engine and got out of the Jeep. If she remembered correctly, this house was over six thousand square feet, with eight bedrooms and a massive living area.

She remembered the boat house, too, with every type of lake toy you could ask for. The boat house sat to the left of the main house. It also had living quarters, and back in its heyday, a caretaker and his family made it their home. It looked newer than the main house, and Libby seemed to recall it had taken extensive damage from the famous storm of 1989.

The property was a riot of color, even early in the season.

Libby spied hydrangea bushes on the cusp of their first bloom. She inhaled the fragrance of the lilac bushes that reached near to the roof of the boat house. Her mood lifted at the site of the vibrant yellow bursting from the early-blooming forsythia bushes. It was a riot of foliage but also threatened to overtake the property. She wondered if her aunt had a gardener anymore.

Despite the color riot, it was actually quiet. The only sound was the lake. She heard the waters lap against the dock.

It felt oddly empty here. This place was made to be filled with kids, families, summer.

It was built for that reason. Her great grandparents designed it as a family escape from the summer heat of Detroit. That city was only an hour away but seemed like another planet.

She looked out at the lake again. Libby longed to walk out on the dock. She wanted to kick off her shoes and put her toes in the water.

But she better go inside, find Aunt Emma, and try to get reacquainted.

They were going to be roomies, she guessed.

She knocked on the door and waited. Getting from one end of the house to another was a hike, not taken quickly. And Aunt Emma probably wasn't moving too fast these days.

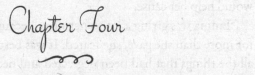

Chapter Four

Emma

She stared at the lake. It was still. The sun made things seem more like summer than spring right now.

That was good. Mother Nature knew that it was best to cooperate with Emma's plans. As should Libby.

The old aluminum raft bobbed gently in the water off the dock. Emma knew the indoor-outdoor carpet on the thing ought to be replaced, but the idea was to remind her niece of the old days. Having that raft out would do the trick.

The sun glinted off the water, and for a moment, Emma could see the girls. All five of them, shoulder to shoulder, on that old raft.

They were giggling about something. Their long limbs were well past being burnt; the summer had turned them all various shades of gold.

Emma loved it when they were all here.

The Sandbar Sisters. So named for their favorite spot to anchor the pontoon.

Emma blinked. That was a memory from a long time ago. No one was on the raft today.

Thank goodness she'd had Patrick hire someone to put the dock in and float the raft. It made the place look less abandoned. It would help her cause.

Emma was giving a lot to her niece because she would soon ask for more than she gave, she feared. It was best that Libby didn't see all the things that had been neglected and needed work. The dock, the boathouse, the guest cottage—the entire town.

Yes, well, at least the dock was in, and the raft was floating.

"Patrick, is the tea ready?"

Patrick was her lawyer, her helper, her driver, her confidant. If Patrick Tate wasn't here to help her, this would have all seemed nearly impossible.

It was good to be friends with a man like Patrick Tate. She insisted he not retire until her plans were sewn up.

Today, Patrick made sure the tea was on. Emma's attorney knew, just like Mother Nature, that it was best to cooperate with her plans.

"Yes, Miss Emma. It is all set out."

"Can you make yourself busy? I want to talk to my niece for a bit."

"Of course."

Patrick was a decade younger than Emma, but sometimes he seemed older than Emma. He was a throwback to another era. Emma liked that about him.

What was taking that girl so long? Emma had seen her drive up, for pity's sake.

Emma wasn't fast on her feet, so she decided to start her careful walk to the door. At her age, careful walking was a matter of self-preservation. Just like taking her nitro and doing her morning stretches.

Finally, there was a knock at the screen.

"Aunt Emma? It's Libby."

Emma opened the door, and there she was. Her beautiful niece. The leader of the pack, or was it a gaggle?

Either way, Libby was a person other people listened to. She was outspoken, bold, smart, and funny. Or she used to be.

The woman at the door was a bit timid. She was also a lot thinner than she ought to be.

"Elizabeth! So glad you're here!" Emma gestured for Libby to come in, and she put out a hand to her niece.

"Libby, please, no one calls me Elizabeth."

Libby took Emma's hand in hers and smiled. Ah, there it was, the smile. Boys used to sniff around this place all summer hoping for Elizabeth—uh, Libby—to bestow it upon them. Emma remembered that, too.

Emma pulled her niece into a careful hug, which was gently returned. Everyone thought Emma was going to crack in half these days. That was bothersome.

"Youth Dew! I forgot that was your scent."

"I had to learn how to order it online. The closest department store is in Ann Arbor, and I'm not driving there just for perfume."

"It smells lovely."

"Thank you."

Libby walked into the house. Emma knew the house was magic. She knew it might be the best place on earth; well, the best place in the summer anyway. But to watch her niece rediscover that was a treat.

"That view, it's unbelievable."

Emma kept her mouth shut. There was no need to clutter up the moment with idle prattle.

Libby walked from the foyer through the small hallway into the huge sitting room, where window after window framed the lake, from corner to corner. The view only stopped when the water met the sky.

"Wow." Libby drank it in for another second.

While the view distracted her niece, Emma took a closer look.

She'd been accurate in her initial assessment of her niece's weight. Where were those muscles she used to have?

The hair was a little bit of a disaster too. Emma could see gray peeking through. Which was fine with Emma. She, too, had been white-haired before it was fashionable. But Libby's hair looked neglected. It had been her crowning glory! Emma got the impression that the rubber band holding Libby's hair in a tight ponytail at the base of her neck was actually holding her entire being together. If Emma snatched that elastic band out of the Libby's hair, her niece's life force would scatter all over the wood floors!

"I've made some tea. And some cucumber sandwiches." A lie, Patrick had made the tea, and she'd ordered the sandwiches from a caterer in nearby Manchester. It was all part of the gracious host act Emma had worked up.

"Oh, that's lovely."

"By the looks of you, I should have made several. You're too skinny."

"Ha, you know, I've had a rough go, the last few, uh, few weeks. Nervous stomach. And you're not supposed to comment on a woman's weight."

"Nonsense, your mother's passed away. If not me, who?"

Libby laughed at that. Her laugh was low, always had been. So was her voice. Maybe that's what made her a leader among those girls. Her voice gave her an air of authority.

"Here."

The two walked to the breakfast nook and sat down.

"This is the same table," Libby said.

"Of course, it's a classic. It can't be replaced."

"It is, truly."

Libby sipped her tea and picked at the sandwiches, cut into triangles. Emma took a good hearty bite. She'd have to lead by example. No man, woman, or checkbook balance was going to stop her from having a delicious sandwich.

"I appreciate you inviting me to visit. I need a little, uh, time off."

"I am not inviting you to visit. I'm leaving this place to you. Papers are already signed. Just like I wrote."

Emma held back. Maybe it was best not to spring the whole story on her at once. Maybe it was best for the lake house to work its way back into Libby's heart.

Emma rarely second-guessed herself, but her instinct told her to hang on a bit. Libby was taking tiny bites of the sandwich. Emma's truth needed to be doled out in tiny bites, too.

"Why me, and why now?"

"First of all, you're the only one in the family with big enough shoulders. This place needs someone to take command!"

"Like you did?"

"Of course, like I did."

"But why now?"

"Are you blind? I'm old as dirt. It's fifteen years past time someone helps me with this place. My heart's bad, my eyes are bad, my doctor says my bones are made of powder, one wrong step, and I'm a goner."

"Oh, you seem pretty hearty right about now."

"Still, the law of averages says I'll not live forever. And let's be honest. You're in a pickle. Aren't you?"

"Ah, yes. You know?"

"They stopped printing the daily paper, but Patrick showed me how to get the "internets". I watched you on the news."

"Great."

"You're not the first woman to be swindled by a no-good, low-down husband."

"Yeah, well, he didn't swindle me. He swindled our entire community. I can't show my face, can't get a job, can't—"

Libby was about to cry. Emma could see that. She could also see that Libby wasn't the crying type. She pulled her emotions back in, back down. She swallowed them, and it looked to Emma like that was the only nourishment the poor thing was getting.

"Swallowing despair does not have the recommended daily requirements of vitamins and minerals," Emma remarked.

Libby laughed loud this time, really guffawed. Emma felt victorious at the sound.

"I'm going to choke on my sandwich!" Libby wiped the corners of her lips. They were a little lined around the edges, but full. The joy of her youth was hiding, not gone, Emma had glimpsed it for a brief second.

"How about this. You spend a day or two here. Resting. Relaxing. Eating, hopefully. And then we'll worry about the details of all this. Patrick!"

Libby jumped a bit in her seat at the sound of Emma's commands.

"My lawyer, he's going to drive me back."

"Back?"

"I live in Silver Estates, east of Adrian, awful name, like Geritol Village or something."

"I thought you lived here?"

"It's too big, too much. My osteoperwhatsits and all."

"Osteoporosis," Libby said.

"Yes, that. And other issues. Silver Estates is for mature adults who might die at the drop of a hat. The entire place is a medical alert bracelet."

"Oh, okay, that seems safer for you for sure."

"Also, Tuesday night is Bingo night. I cannot miss it." Emma wasn't kidding about that. There would be issues if Rose Brubaker got Emma's favorite seat in the community room.

Patrick appeared with Emma's sweater.

"The keys to everything from boats to boathouses are in the drawer next to the refrigerator," Emma instructed. "I've stocked it with a few staples, but you'll probably want to take a trip to Peck's

—that's still there. They don't have everything, but they do have a decent selection of grocery store wine and cheese."

Libby looked at her like she was speaking in tongues. "I, uh, okay."

"If a store has good wine and cheese, it's a good store."

"Yes, agree, one hundred percent."

Libby looked confused, which was to be expected. Imagine how confused she'll be in a few days. Imagine how angry.

Yes, Emma thought it was good to give her niece a day or two here. The woman needed it. She needed sleep. She needed food. She needed to not worry.

At least for a few days.

The worries were there, waiting.

Patrick looked at Emma with a question in his eyes. He knew she'd planned to unfurl the whole thing, but she gave him a slight nod. *No. Not now.*

Patrick helped her up and held her cardigan for her.

Libby stood up too. "Ugh, so keys in the drawer, anything else I need to know?"

"The dock's in. There's some gas in the boat, right?'"

Patrick nodded yes.

"Okay, and uh, you'll be back when?"

"How about two days? You rest up. Let the lake air fix you up for a day or two. And then we'll talk."

"Okay, sure, I can't thank you enough. I think you're right. A few days of just being here, at peace, will do me some good."

Libby looked lighter in the eyes. *Aha, see, my sparkly niece was buried in there, trying to come to the surface.*

"You're down. But you're not out. I've been both. I know." Emma squeezed Libby's shoulder.

"Okay, yes, you're right. You're right."

And tears sparkled in the corners of Libby's eyes. Her beautiful, strong niece was fierce, the right kind of fierce that Irish Hills needed.

"Of course."

"Yes, worry-free, I like it." Emma left it at that. Emma and Patrick walked to the door. She would give Libby a little space to pull herself together.

Once they were out of earshot, Patrick scolded Emma.

"She's going to have to know what you've done, sooner rather than later," Patrick said.

"I know, I know. She needs to gather her strength, though."

"Yes, ma'am. Back to your place?"

"And on the way, we need to stop at Meijer's. I told Rose I'd bring the cheesecake tonight, and she is a real pill when she doesn't have desert."

Patrick nodded yes, and they drove away from the lake house.

Yes, Emma thought, *Libby needs a few worry-free days. But I can only afford to give her a few.*

The strings that Emma had attached to this deal were more like chains that would pull them both down to the bottom of Lake Manitou, house and all, if she was wrong about the fight left in Libby Quinn.

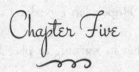

Chapter Five

Libby

Libby rolled her larger suitcase and matching small suitcase into the house.

She was alone, maybe for the first time, in this space.

Her mind flashed to a long-ago slumber party, back when they first met Viv.

1985, Nora House

"You're looking ill," Libby said to Hope.

"You're looking pale," J.J. said.

Hope collapsed in a dramatic heap in the center of them. Hope's oversized INXS concert t-shirt came to the knees of what was supposed to be a lifeless body.

"Oh, oh no!" Viv said. She was the youngest. This was all for her benefit. She sounded skeptical and slightly concerned at the same time.

The four girls who weren't dead put two fingers at the four corners of the spectacularly dead Hope.

Libby could see Hope's left eye trying to sneak a peek at the drama around her.

Libby pinched her in warning to play along. She started the chant.

"Light as a feather, stiff as a board; light as a feather, stiff as a board."

She and Hope were the same age and had summer birthdays. They always had a slumber party to celebrate.

J.J. and Goldie joined in. They'd been through this little exercise before. Viv followed suit.

The four girls lifted, lifted, lifted. Maybe they would have actually achieved magical levitation if it weren't for Hope forgetting to be dead.

She squealed and doubled over in laughter.

Busted!

"I knew we should have had Goldie be the dead one. She's the actress," J.J. said.

J.J. was right. Goldie *was* the actress.

Goldie made a gesture. Her Sun In enhanced yellow locks framed her face as she struck the pose.

"I KNEW it was totally bogus, *knew* it!" Viv said. She was the newest of their gang. Turns out she was also the savviest to slumber party games.

* * *

Libby could almost hear the laughter that resulted in the failed attempt at Light as a Feather. She knew what had happened to Goldie. Everyone on the planet knew. But Hope, JJ, and Viv? She had lost touch with them after that summer in 1989. Being here reminded her. They were the best friends she'd ever had.

And they'd let each other go.

Libby shook off the memories and looked for a place to set up.

The main bedroom had always been Aunt Emma's. Libby decided that it was way too forward to take her aunt's room. She knew Aunt Emma said this house was to be hers. But still, it seemed obnoxious and a sign that she agreed with her aunt's nutty assertions to claim the primary suite. If Aunt Emma had stayed, Libby would have taken Patrick Tate aside and fired off some questions about her aunt's offer.

No matter. She'd rest for a couple days, free of charge and free of responsibility. And then, if her aunt continued to insist this house was hers, Libby would corner the lawyer.

While the main bedroom was the biggest, there were plenty of others to choose from.

Libby scouted the one that her parents had used when they visited.

A queen-sized bed was against one wall. It faced a triple bank of floor-to-ceiling French doors, which opened up to a little patio. The room also had an ensuite bathroom. This was about as perfect as a bedroom got, Libby decided.

This place was built one-hundred years ago, but it had been upgraded with bathrooms and electricity in the 1970s. Despite the many design fads of that era, Aunt Emma had clearly seen to it that nothing was trendy here. Everything was classic. Libby admired that discipline.

This would do nicely, she decided.

Libby wheeled her bags into the room. She wasn't unpacking anything else. She really didn't know how long this was going to last.

Two days of just being here, not looking forward, and no stress over what had just passed in her life, was going to be her mission.

She opened the French doors and walked out on the patio. A glass of wine, a cup of coffee, a good book; this was the place for all of it.

She inhaled the clean air. Her breath caught, and out of nowhere, she started to cry.

Libby was used to stifling her tears. She saw it as her duty to keep it together for everyone else. *I haven't got time for the pain...*

She let go of her natural instinct to rein it all in. Alone on the patio, with the glassy lake in front of her and the foundation of the house solid underneath her, she let the tears flow.

For a good minute or two, Libby released whatever this was—sadness, regret, frustration? Probably all of the above. And then she wiped her cheeks. It was the first time she'd cried in all these months. She'd clenched her teeth, she'd smashed the sign, she'd balled her fists, but all of that was to stop the tears. Here, she let them out. And then they stopped.

Libby collected herself. Her heart felt somehow calmer. Lighter.

She was currently wearing tailored dress pants, a silk blouse, and a neat blazer. It was pulled together. She liked being pulled together. Or used to. Now it seemed ridiculous. She wasn't here to impress anyone. Her days of aiming to impress with chic style were over. Now, she just wanted to be comfortable.

"What kind of lake attire is this? I look like I'm running for office," Libby said aloud and did not mind hearing her own voice in the space.

She opened her suitcase found a pair of jeans, a white t-shirt, and a pair of top siders.

She put on the t-shirt and shoes and scooped up the jeans. She padded back to the kitchen and opened several drawers until she found them.

"Aha! The good scissors!"

There were good scissors, and there were bad scissors. You kept the bad ones around but honored and protected the good ones like a holy relic. These scissors were good and had been here for decades.

Libby placed the jeans on the counter and eyeballed the length; definitely a few more inches were required since the last time she'd done this particular denim surgery.

She cut the jeans off and turned them into shorts. She shimmied into her new creation. The jeans were already broken in, loose even, given her recent unplanned weight loss. They were the perfect attire for the next few days.

Libby looked down at her legs.

"Oh, lord, I need some self-tanner." Normally, she slathered on the sunscreen. But what harm could a few hours in the April sun of Michigan do? Her legs might be white as snow, but there were long, muscular, and had been holding her up just fine despite the weight of her current predicament.

She grabbed a fleece pullover, too, just in case, and set out for the lake to get a little sun.

After a couple of attempts, she found the right key for the boathouse. The doors creaked as she yanked them open.

She remembered where the light switch was like she was there last year.

She clicked it up, and the fluorescents that hung from the ceiling of the exposed beam structure flickered on.

She screamed and jumped back. A cobweb the size of a bed sheet wrapped itself over her face before she realized it was there.

Libby choked down her initial reaction. She brushed off the webbing and took another step inside.

A pontoon boat dominated the space. A broad smile and little laugh came just as easily as the tears had earlier.

The *S.S. Lazy Dayz* had been the site of a lot of shenanigans. She'd taken it out to their sandbar many times. In the 1980s, a boater's safety certification was mandatory in schools in Michigan.

She'd learned it like CPR. Could she still drive this thing? Did it even work? Well, it didn't matter, it was in the boat house. She had no way to tow it to the water.

The same was true for the little speed boat. Both were more complicated projects than she had the bandwidth for today.

There was a kayak, a canoe, and even a pedal boat. All were workable. And maybe tomorrow morning, she'd try the kayak. She wanted a cruise now, though, not a workout.

Maybe this wasn't going to happen, not without some help.

She scanned the walls. There were flags of various types, a croquet set, a deadly as heck lawn jart set, archery stuff. All of it had provided hours of fun when she was a kid.

The water skis also caught her eye. She wondered again about that activity.

Likely she wouldn't be here long enough to try, and well, she had zero friends to help her with that experiment.

She closed the door, locked it up, and decided to walk out to the dock.

As she did, she saw the perfect solution for her desire to get out on the water.

There it was: the old outboard fishing boat. Her dad spent most of his lake time on this boat with her brother. Libby had eschewed it for skiing and tanning when she was a teen. But not when she was a little kid. She knew how to do this. She was sure of it.

Libby looked back at the house. Her aunt had to have arranged for the dock, the raft, and the little boat to be in the water. It really was the perfect boat for her to have her one-woman tour.

Libby surveyed the contents of the boat. There was an old orange lifejacket and a paddle if it stalled out. There was a net for hauling in the fish, but she wasn't planning on trying to catch anything. Two boards were positioned across the width of the boat to sit on.

The thing looked solid and seaworthy, so Libby decided to go for it.

She climbed in carefully. She reached around to the rope that started the portable outboard motor. Libby gave it a yank. Nothing. She did it again. Nothing.

And then she remembered the trick to it. She was going to have to be a bit more serious about that yank.

She did it again, and the motor sputtered to life.

Victory!

She watched water spit out the back. *Good, good.* It was go time. She unhitched the dock lines and gripped the tiller tightly. Libby was exhilarated. She used to do this all the time!

She didn't think much about anything else, just slowly taking a tour of Lake Manitou. She knew the rules of the lake. She knew where a wake was allowed and where it wasn't. But honestly, the place was fairly deserted. On a holiday weekend, she would have had to be more careful. She knew boat traffic was nuts out here then.

But right now, anyway, she had the lake to herself. She'd skirt the perimeter slowly and just take it all in.

Libby cruised slowly past a few nearby cottages. They were likely empty this early. Most of the people here weren't year-round residents—or they weren't back in her day.

There were older cottages, ones she remembered, looking a bit like the guest cottage on Sandy Beach Lane. But then there were others that looked brand new.

As she continued to take in the scene, Libby was astonished to see several stunning homes. To call them cottages was like calling Nora House a cottage. They were mansions on the water, no question about it.

She wondered if any of the old families she knew were still here. She wondered if Hope, J.J., or the rest of the gang ever came back.

J.J. was from Irish Hills. Maybe she'd even stayed on?

Libby passed a couple of old-timers in a boat that was not too different from the one she was in. They'd cast their lines in the water. She slowed down and swung wide and to the right. She knew the etiquette. Libby wasn't there to disturb their fishing hole. She waved, they waved back.

She was completely across the lake now and looked back where she came from. One summer, she'd made it her mission to swim across. She couldn't imagine it now; it gave her a backache to think about.

Libby planned to skirt the other side of the lake on the way back to Nora House, maybe even head toward the little channel and see what Round Lake looked like.

But then the boat engine sputtered.

"Don't you even," Libby said.

It sputtered again and died.

"Crap."

Libby twisted around. She pulled the cord, once, twice, three times. Nothing.

She remembered then that this happened. It always happened. But she had always had backup or a bathing suit.

She put her hand in the water. It was ice cold. No. No swimming home today.

She was in a pickle now, adrift at the far side of the lake.

The oars for emergencies were there, sitting at the bottom of the boat.

Libby wasn't convinced she'd be able to paddle it back across the big lake to the house.

She sat, annoyed at her overconfidence.

"This is your own fault," she said to the fish that boldly swam by. How did they know she wasn't in a position to catch them right now?

She floated a little longer and decided she better start paddling.

She got the oars in the water and tried to remember the motion.

As she did, a boat approached. The wake of it caused her own to pitch a bit.

"Whoa!" she said as she tried not to dump.

A man in a well-warn Tigers baseball hat, similarly beat-up jeans, and a t-shirt that read *Steve's Marina* stood behind the steering wheel.

"You need a tow?"

The sun was behind him. He was in shadow, but Libby had to shield her eyes.

"I need my head examined is what I need. This was not one of my more well thought out ideas."

The man laughed.

"Out of gas?"

Libby realized that she hadn't even checked that, hadn't Patrick the lawyer said there was gas? She'd been so thrilled that the motor had started she hadn't thought about whether there was enough gas to go swanning around Lake Manitou for an hour.

"Probably." Either that or the old motor was clogged or out of oil or any number of mundane boat calamities.

The man in the Steve's Marina t-shirt expertly inched his boat closer to hers.

"Throw me your line. I'll tow you."

"Really, thank you, yes, that would be so great."

Libby reached for the line. And she prayed she could toss it without taking a swim when she did.

She coiled it, eyeballed the man's boat, and hoped for the best. He reached out and grabbed it. It was like they'd done this maneuver a million times.

"Nice yeet," the man said.

"You clearly have a teen in your life," Libby said. Yeet was a kid word, not a grown-up word.

"I work with too many of 'em," he laughed. It was an easy laugh. And it sparked something.

A memory. A moment.

She looked again. The sun and that ball cap made it hard to see his face. But the way he looked in those jeans. Libby could scarcely believe it. She realized she and this man *had* done this a million times.

Or at least a hundred, but not since that summer in 1989.

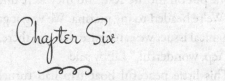

Chapter Six

Libby

The hoisting of a full-grown woman from a fishing boat to a much larger boat might be the least graceful thing any woman can do. Much less a woman of a certain age.

It may have been years since Libby was on these waters, but she was no dummy. She didn't want to go through that humiliation. Things were embarrassing enough already. Nope, she'd stay perched in her bum boat while her would-be rescuer towed them.

Luckily, her rescuer was on the same page with towing instead of hauling her onto his boat.

"It's going to be slow going, and regs say you need your life vest on."

"I'm sure it's fine I can—"

"It's a safety thing, safety first, young lady."

"Young lady? Yeah, maybe I better put the thing on. You're clearly visually impaired."

"What?"

Oh good, he hadn't heard her sarcastic reply. She had to

remember people were just nicer here. Her biting comments would have sharper teeth to their ears. And he was doing her a huge favor.

She put on the life vest, and they were underway.

"We're headed to my marina. We've got gas if that's it or if it's a mechanical issue, we can figure that out there, too."

"Yep, wonderful," Libby said.

This little peaceful boat trip had turned into an episode of *This is Your Life*. Libby imagined she looked a fright with her windblown hair, shorts she'd hacked off herself, ratty t-shirt, and of course, she felt the sting of sunburn on every bit of exposed skin.

This was not how she'd have selected to look when running into this particular old friend.

Well, more than friend. On the other hand, it had been decades. She'd aged. She didn't look the same. Maybe he wouldn't recognize her.

While the memory of the last time she'd seen him was burned into her brain, resurfacing now as they made their way to the marina, she realized he probably didn't think of her at all.

He looked fit, more filled out than the lanky teenager he'd been, but in a good way. From back in the day, Libby remembered his heartthrob smile and amber-colored eyes that she had thought were dreamy. Yet somehow, he looked even better now, from what she could see. Because, men.

The trip to the marina was lightning fast, in Libby's estimation. Mainly because her brain was working overtime.

When they got to the docks of Steve's Marina, she remembered it. This place was called Steve's way back in her day, too. Though surely Steve himself must be retired. Her would-be rescuer expertly docked his boat, tied it quickly, and grabbed the tether to hers.

She tried not to notice how easy it was for him to haul her and the boat into the dock.

Libby grabbed one piling so as not to crash. He put a hand out at the other end of the boat, and they barely dinged the bumpers.

He did this all the time.

"Good job putting in," he complimented her.

Okay, well, that was something. Now to just smoothly get out of here and back to the lake house without this turning weird.

Libby wanted to leap from the boat to anywhere on the planet, but instead, she knew she best take the hand that was offered to her. She did so, reluctantly. Strong forearms were highly underrated when it came to evaluating the attractiveness of a man.

"You're not used to taking help, are you?"

"Uh, no."

He hauled her up to the dock and pulled her off balance, just a little. She fell into him for a nano second. They were face to face, inches away. She saw him up close now. He had a few wrinkles, a little stubble, but Libby's initial assessment was right. The cute boy had grown into a ruggedly sexy man.

Wow.

His amber eyes locked into hers, and he remembered. Libby saw his eyes change as he figured out who this damn damsel was.

"It can't be! Libby? You look the same. How did I not see?"

"Hi, Keith."

Keith Brady, a former friend, turned boyfriend, turned, uh— Libby stopped her train of thoughts. Hopefully, she wasn't blushing. She was too old to blush.

He held her hand a moment longer, and she removed it, awkwardly to be sure.

"Wow, I never thought I'd see you back here."

"I didn't know you still lived here. It looks like you took over Steve's old place."

"Yeah, boat docking, repair, winter storage, all of it. Bought it from Steve, actually."

"Lucky for me."

"I just can't believe you're here—and getting a nasty sunburn, it appears." Keith had looked down to see Libby's previously white legs that looked shockingly pink now.

"Oh, it's nothing, just building a base, you know."

He laughed. She remembered now. Her jokes worked on him. And vice versa. That was a thing they had.

"What are you doing here?"

"Uh, my aunt invited me. I needed a few days R & R, so you know, floundering in the lake without gas is my self-care plan."

"Right, right, better than a spa day. How about you get out of the sun, grab some water or a pop, and I'll check this out. See if you're out of gas or out of luck."

"Great, yes, and thank you for the tow. I was about ready to swim for it."

"You could do it. You've got great shoulders, always have."

Libby, usually fast with the quip, had none to offer. Her answer was an unexpected throwback to the Libby of 1980-something. "Shut *upppp*!"

She'd not seen this man in decades, he'd helped her out of a tight spot, and she felt comfortable enough to tell him to shut up.

Ugh. Not cool, she thought. She decided getting in the marina and collecting herself might be a very good idea.

Libby left Keith to do whatever with her aunt's boat. She didn't dare glance back. Or say something else stupid. She worried all of a sudden what her butt looked like. *Snap out of it, Quinn, no one is looking at your butt.*

Libby walked into the old marina building, and it too was looking very good. And it was still attached to a restaurant, though that looked less updated. Maybe it was closed?

Libby found the restroom and dealt with her hair as best as possible. Grabbing a water was not as easily done. She'd left the house without a purse or phone or brain, apparently. She didn't even have a couple of quarters to use the vending machine.

Instead, Libby explored the marina a bit. She was incredibly curious, all of a sudden, about Keith's current situation. She poked into an office, it was empty, but the door was open. That wasn't too forward, was it?

It looked like he had a great life here. There were pictures showing friends, a beautiful woman in his arms in several, and a few shots of teenagers in football uniforms adorning the walls behind his desk. There was also a picture of Keith in fatigues.

He was a vet.

So, he hadn't been here the whole time. Libby felt a pang of guilt that she didn't know anything about Keith's life until this very moment.

"Looks like we need to do some work on that outboard of yours."

Libby jumped a foot in the air. She tried to cover, but she was snooping in this man's office. No way around that.

"Oh, oh, okay, sure. I mean, it's not mine. It's Aunt Emma's. I'm going to have to see what she wants done with it."

"Well, let me give you a lift back to Nora House. That's where you are, right?"

"Yes, but, uh, that's not necessary. I can walk or Uber or—"

"City girl, the Uber here is called 'hit up your neighbor'. You've been gone way too long. Come on, I'll drive you back."

Libby realized he was right, and her weirdness was on her. She accessed the part of her comfortable in command and stopped being so girlish.

"Thank you, of course."

They got into a meticulously restored vintage blue truck with the marina logo and phone number stenciled on both sides.

"You haven't been here forever, and you're visiting now? What's up in your life, Libby?"

"Oh, just...it's great. Three grown kids. In between jobs, but uh, great."

Libby felt like she was at a high school reunion and had nothing to show for her life. Her current situation was way too complicated to convey in small talk. *Hi, I recently didn't get charged with a felony, and my kids are geniuses AND gorgeous. How about you?*

How did you catch someone up on thirty years?

"Hey, I've got three also, three sons."

"Two daughters and son here." Okay, all this was good, nice, and manageable surface chit-chat.

"But you're on your own for this visit?"

"Uh, to be honest, I've had a bit of a rough patch of late. Needed a few days to get it together, you know, that's how it goes."

What did Keith know? It looked like his life was picture-perfect.

"It does go that way sometimes. Last I heard, you were in Chicago."

"I was, yes, my husband and I—uh my ex-husband—um, we raised the kids in the suburbs there, yes."

"So, no more Henry."

"Right." Desperate to change the subject, Libby turned the conversation to Keith's business. "The marina looks like it's doing well."

"Yeah, it's good. My sons work with me, well, two of the three. The youngest is deployed overseas right now."

"That sounds pretty great." Sons probably meant wife. She had spied and seen the picture of a pretty woman in Keith's arms. The mother of those three handsome sons. Libby felt a pang of regret that their two lives had diverged so completely.

"It was," Keith said. "It is."

"Working with your wife and kids, that's the dream, right?" Libby was trying to fill dead air, trying to pretend she wasn't flustered by running into Keith Brady.

"Yes, my late wife, she passed a couple of years ago."

Now Libby felt like a complete jerk for forcing Keith to tell her that. She was small and insensitive.

"I'm so sorry."

"Thank you, we're doing okay. Miss her, though."

"I saw her picture in your office, beautiful."

"Yep. She was."

Keith had lived a whole life, one with joy and pain, just like she had. She hated that she'd missed it. They were once so close.

"And those sons are mighty handsome, if I do say so."

"Thank you. Here's the real question, though, any red heads in that brood of yours?"

The dark little cloud passed over and out of their space. Libby felt the blush creep up again. It was the way he said it. He used to say he loved her hair. She remembered that. She also put her hand up to it reflexively. It was a sight, she knew. The red locks needed a lot of help to stay red these days.

"My youngest girl has my hair, for sure, the other two, blondes." She almost said, "Blondes like their dad," but cut herself off. She was trying not to bring Henry into this little reunion. A bit of awkwardness sat between them on the bench seat of the truck now. It might be decades of water under the bridge, but Henry had come between them. No two ways around it. She'd let Henry, actually. Libby was as much to blame as Henry in what happened with Keith.

"Here we are." They pulled into Sandy Beach Lane, and she did not venture a look at the guest cottage as they passed, not with Keith sitting right there. Nope.

"Thank you again. What do I owe you? My wallet is inside."

"Nothing, don't worry about it. How about I just swing by in a few days and bring your aunt up to speed on the situation with the boat, see what she wants to be done."

"You know, you can probably call her at Silver Estates. I'm not going to be here long, and I have no idea how she handles that sort of thing."

"Okay, sure." He looked a little stung, or maybe Libby's sixteen-year-old imagination had taken over.

"Good seeing you," Libby said.

"Hey, you check in on J.J.? She'd love to hear from you, I bet."

"She's still in town?"

"Never left, rents a booth at Hairdo or Dye. Maybe you'd like to visit her for a couple reasons." And the son of a gun pointed to the top of his head, indicating Libby's roots.

Libby's jaw dropped, and she tried not to laugh.

"Nice, there's the Keith I knew. Enough of this chivalrous boat rescue jazz," Libby said.

"You'd look good bald. And shut up, yourself." Keith winked, and that was it. He threw the truck into reverse and maneuvered it out of the driveway and out of her sight.

Libby was still blown away.

Keith Brady. Unreal.

Chapter Seven

Libby

Libby spent the next couple of days sleeping, walking, and reminiscing. Not about the scandal and how she'd failed. But about how when she was here, in this place, during those summers, it was all ahead of her.

Her potential had stretched out in front of her like an endless sunrise.

She was always what people called a "go-getter" when they were being nice. Or "bossy" when they were trying to cut her down. But the put-downs didn't work to keep her from speaking up. She didn't shy away from the word bossy. She didn't recoil from raising her hand when she knew the answer or directing the group projects.

She'd taken that attitude through her adult life, and up until a year ago, it had worked out, or so she thought.

But now, all her mistakes, including the ones she made the last summer she was here, ran through her head.

She thought a little about Henry and how she'd let herself get in a position to be so blind. Was it because she'd gotten too sure of herself? Was she cocky?

It was a line that men didn't have to walk. A balance beam they were never on, so they didn't risk falling off. They could be cocky. They weren't bossy. They were the boss.

Thankfully, when her doubts and regrets—and quite frankly, heartache—got too oppressive, the lake provided the needed distraction.

When the emotions of the last year darkened her mood, she went outside. She removed cobwebs from every square inch of the main house. She trimmed back some of the bushes. She washed two dozen windows. It was good exercise, but better still, it pulled her out of the pit she'd been in since Chicago. She felt a bit of optimism nudge out the despair one little task at a time.

For the two days she had, alone at Nora House, Libby didn't go into town or drive anywhere. She didn't check her social media or scan her email. She looked no farther than the water. She stood still and watched the ducks swim by with their fuzzy yellow ducklings trailing behind them.

She stayed in the now. The last year felt less like a weight around her neck and more like a place she'd driven out of, a landmark of her life that was getting smaller in the rearview mirror.

She woke up early on the first day of May.

It was still quiet on the lake. The true busy season was only a few weeks away. Memorial Day was the kickoff. She suspected that the warmer than typical spring weather had lured some cottage owners back early, though. She'd noticed a slight uptick in boat traffic.

The motorboat excursion might have been a debacle, but it hadn't deterred Libby from wanting to get out on the water.

She put on her bathing suit, a life jacket, and decided a little bit of kayaking was in order before she left today.

It was dawn. She carefully got in the kayak and began to paddle. In only a few strokes, she was underway, the sleek profile of the kayak sliced through the glassy surface. Libby had the hang of it quickly. She alternated strokes, one side and then the other. She pushed the water with the paddle and relished her ability to control the speed and direction. There was no wind. That was key, she knew. Wind could turn ten minutes out into two hours back.

Libby paused her strokes. She looked toward the lake house. It stood on the small hill of the peninsula, like a queen. She imagined her great grandmother, Nora herself, taking in this view. What went through her mind back then?

Nora Sullivan was a house-maid who'd married a rich man, Libby's great grandfather. He'd built this place for her. The story went that she refused to hire a maid to clean it. She insisted she and her girls do it themselves. Libby knew how much time that must have taken now that she'd done the thing herself that last few days.

Libby was halfway across the lake now.

The kayak rocked a bit in the water. Libby stopped trying to move things forward, perfect her stroke, or get somewhere else. She floated in place, the kayak bobbing on the current she'd only just stopped creating.

Libby took everything in. She'd been paddling so long, so hard, to get somewhere.

Libby looked up at the pink sky, dotted with a few gray puffs of clouds.

A light mist hung low around the trees that circled the lake. A flock of geese flew overhead.

She settled her breathing after the effort of paddling out here.

Libby heard a red-winged blackbird trilling from the nearby cattails.

She had no idea how long she just floated there, and let the water decide the direction. But it was enough to calm her heart and mind.

She put her paddle in the water again to start her journey back to the dock.

This time she moved slower. She'd be at the dock and back to the real world soon enough.

The soundtrack to this meditation was the gentle swish of her paddle through the water, one side, and then the other. She heard the bird call, and her breath.

Libby had tried to meditate before but could never find the well of patience it required or time. But she suspected this was it. This was what she had been after, a stillness of mind that had eluded her until now.

Aunt Emma was set to visit for lunch, and Libby figured that would be the end of her time here. She was grateful for it. She had done a lot of healing just by being here, just by putting her feet on the sandy beach at the end of the lawn.

She was looking forward to seeing her aunt and thanking her for the surprise sanctuary. But she was packed and ready to set out, though she didn't know where.

Her aunt's assertion that she'd left Libby this house was, well, batty. That said, Libby was rested, somewhat restored, and certainly possessed with a better outlook than when she came.

She needed a job, a more permanent place to live, and a restart. But this detour to the lake of her childhood had cleared the literal and metaphysical cobwebs. It had put her on the right foot for the next part of her life.

Chapter Eight

Emma

Her niece had enjoyed two full days of relaxation. Two days to appreciate Nora House, and the lake, and the opportunity that was at her feet.

Patrick had picked Emma up and was at the ready with the details they had planned to spring on Libby the first day.

Emma couldn't wait any longer.

She found her niece placing a tray of food out on the back porch.

"Where did you find this table and chair set?"

"Your boathouse is filled with treasures. Is it okay to sit out here? Too chilly?"

"No, my cardigan is here, and it's fine, just fine."

"Wonderful."

Libby Quinn looked a damn sight better. The shadow moons under her eyes were gone. And she looked fuller, less gaunt. Emma hoped her niece felt less defeated, less haunted. The lake had produced the desired effect, Emma determined.

She needed Libby to be full strength.

"How have you found the place?"

"Aunt Emma, it's just as beautiful as I remember. More. I went for a ride in the old fishing boat, cleaned up this table and chair—hope you don't mind that—and just loved sitting by the water. Truly, just what I needed."

"Good, good. And, of course, I don't mind. It's yours anyway."

"That's very sweet of you. You do not have to leave me this place in your will."

Here's where the rubber meets the road, thought Emma.

"I actually want to give it to you now, not later, after I'm gone," Emma stated. "I don't live here, and you belong here."

"I, uh, I can't."

Emma saw the young Libby that swam this lake with confident strokes. She could still see remnants of that bold girl.

Emma pushed. Hopefully, she didn't have to push too hard. But she would.

"Oh, nonsense, I've been a good steward of it forever. It's your turn."

Libby hesitated. Emma watched Libby calculate the pros and cons in her mind as if she'd gotten out a ledger and listed them.

"I'm embarrassed to say this, but I have no income, no savings, no retirement plan. All of it was wiped out, uh, recently."

"Oh, I know. I follow the news. I realize you got royally duped by that Henry Malcolm. Father said, never trust a Malcolm."

Henry Ford had warned Albert Libby. Too bad no one had warned her niece.

"Well, be that as it may, I have no way to pay the taxes here, or insurance, or whatever it costs to heat this thing in the winter. As much as I wish I did."

"I have also set up a trust for all those things you just mentioned. It will be easy as pie for you. I mean, rent out a room in the summer, and you've even got grocery money."

"A trust?"

"Patrick!" Emma called the lawyer, and he materialized. "Explain the house deal to my niece. She's rightly skeptical."

"Miss Emma has set up a trust that will pay for the upkeep of the property, repairs, and insurance. Here's the deed and the documentation." Patrick produced a manilla file folder and slid it in front of Libby.

Libby looked from Patrick to Emma.

Emma was still and quiet. Let the gift speak for itself. She could see her niece thought she'd lost her marbles. She'd see soon enough that her marbles were just fine, thank you.

Libby perused the paperwork. She'd been the CEO of a major charity until recently. She knew how to read legal paperwork, deeds, and documents.

"I, uh, this is amazing."

"I'm giving it to you anyway when I die if you don't sign now. Why not take it today? You're not getting any younger either. Enjoy it. I know you love this place like I do. And I'm still alive. You can have me over, ask me questions, whatever you need."

Patrick produced a pen from his inside pocket.

It was in Libby's hand, smooth as can be.

Libby looked at the lake and gave Emma a glance. Emma smiled back. Appearing benevolent was the order of the day.

Libby put pen to paper and signed.

Emma felt a huge weight lift.

She had her niece exactly where she needed.

And she better get out of here, fast, and get things filed before Libby changed her mind. Deeds didn't transfer themselves!

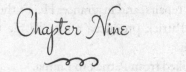

Chapter Nine

Libby

Had she lost her mind? Had the lake lulled her into some sort of stupor and turned her into a person who makes a life decision in a split second? What had just happened?

Her over-ninety-year-old aunt, got up from her chair so fast, that she looked like she was sticking the landing of an Olympic balance beam dismount.

"Wonderful, congratulations, this is wonderful!!" Aunt Emma offered a hand to Libby. Libby took it, and then Aunt Emma came in for a hug. "You've made the best decision of your life. This is your home, always has been."

"Thank you," Libby said. What she wanted to say was, "Did you hypnotize me, old woman?"

Aunt Emma made her way around the back porch to the steps and out to the car pad with almost a skip in her step. "I'm so pleased for you."

"I uh, there's probably a lot I need to know about how to run this place, the boats—oh, on that, the marina has the outboard fishing boat. It needs to have work done; do you want them to—"

"—Dear, they're all yours, the boats, the bats, the badminton." Aunt Emma laughed at her alliteration.

"Oh, okay."

Patrick appeared to have a bit of empathy or maybe sympathy for Libby. She probably looked like she'd been run over by a train and lived to tell about it. Maybe she had. He put a hand on Libby's shoulder. "All the financial and legal documents are in the manilla folder there. Miss Emma also kept a great record of what needs to be done around the house from one of her previous house managers."

"House managers? I don't need a house manager, do I?"

"No, you're young. She didn't get Barney until she was seventy-five because she fell off the roof."

"You *fell off the roof*?"

"I was cleaning the gutters. It happens!" Aunt Emma was in the back seat of the Lincoln Town Car. She'd skipped there like a young girl.

"The bank accounts are all set up, including a debit card and credit card."

"How, I mean, I didn't agree to this until this minute."

"Your aunt likes to be prepared, and no one has ever been able to resist her charm."

The way Patrick said it, Libby had a flash of awareness that maybe her aunt and Patrick had a thing. Wow. A thing? At ninety? Seeing how well her aunt was moving, all of a sudden, Libby didn't think "a thing" was out of the question.

Well, romance springs eternal, it appeared.

"Come on, Patrick, we need to get moving." Aunt Emma clapped her hands together, and Patrick tilted his head in her direction.

But before he did, he turned a kindly eye on Libby. "Yes, you have our number. And your aunt has you visiting day after tomorrow for lunch at Silver Estates."

"Okay, sure, yes," Libby answered this without thinking, as though all of a sudden, she had no free will. *Yes, I'll take the house; yes, I'll meet you; yes, I shall do your bidding.* Her brain was a zombie with arms out in front of her, feet shuffling aimlessly.

Patrick and Aunt Emma drove off.

Libby coughed as the dust from the gravel drive kicked up a cloud behind Aunt Emma's car. It wasn't even noon. Libby had made a massive decision in a mere moment. Normally, she weighed pros and cons, got bids for services, and compared options.

She did not hair-trigger anything. And especially now, in the midst of a crisis of confidence, she should not make any sudden moves. How had she decided to say yes to her aunt's crazy gift? This was like cutting bangs because you had a bad day. It was always prudent to take a beat before cutting those bangs!

But she hadn't. She'd leaped and not looked.

Libby stood, like a statue, in the doorway and blinked several times. She had to be sure she was grounded in reality.

Libby owned the Nora House. What?

Had she just made a colossal, impulsive, crazy mistake? She began to move. Okay good, her limbs work like human limbs. This was progress.

She walked out into the drive. Suddenly, she had concerns about the roof, the gutters, the electrical, the plumbing, the foundation! She hadn't even had it inspected, and she'd signed on the dotted line!

I own the lake house.

Libby walked back into the house, through the kitchen, and into the sitting room that looked out on the lake. The sun was higher in the sky now. It was burning the pink of dawn away.

It was beautiful, and she knew being here the last two days had been a balm to her soul. Just as her aunt said it would be.

Libby put her mind back to the moments before her aunt

arrived, to her morning kayak, to her evening glass of wine on the porch. It had been lovely. Restorative. It had felt like coming home, more than just the place, she'd glimpsed the person she'd been in those far away summers.

That was why Libby trusted her gut and signed the deed. Her aunt had pushed her, for sure, but she'd done it of her own accord. Unless Aunt Emma had slipped a mind-altering drug into the Youth Dew, Libby had to own it. She'd signed. No gun to her head, she'd signed.

She must have wanted to.

Libby reordered her thinking. She wasn't a zombie. She wasn't lacking fee will. Maybe she had just done what she was meant to do, what she needed to do. Maybe she had just gotten out of her own way?

It was okay. She could handle this. It was a house, not a national landmark, for goodness' sake. She could deal with a house.

What was the worst that could happen? If it was a mistake, if she wasn't supposed to be here, to do this, she'd sell the house.

She hated that idea. This house was a part of her family's history.

She'd reveled in the story of her rough and tumble union leader grandfather, Butch Quinn, sweeping Alice Libby, her heiress grandmother, off her feet, on this very porch!

This wasn't a sentence or a trap. It was an opportunity.

What had Aunt Emma said?

Oh yes, that Emma was a steward of this place.

Okay, that was the language that appealed to Libby. She understood community resources, preservation, leaving something better than she found it. It had been her life's work back in Chicago.

She could make this place her home, solve her temporary living situation, and maybe do a few things this summer to fix what needed fixing.

Yes, summer. It wasn't exactly a punishment to stay here for a summer. It made her feel better to think of a season, not forever. It was a season. She could handle a season. Heck, she'd love a season here.

Libby let excitement and optimism edge out the anxiety she'd felt for making a rash decision.

Libby was going to make this work. Maybe it was the right thing at the right time.

And honestly, Libby didn't have anything else pressing to do. No job, grown kids, and AWOL ex-husband.

Libby knew herself well enough to know that sinking her teeth into a project was a great way to lift her mood.

She was a doer, darn it.

She went into the kitchen opened a drawer, near the landline phone. She found a pencil and pad.

She needed groceries, a trip to the hardware store, to call Keith about the boat, and what did Keith say? Oh yeah, she needed her roots done.

That exchange made her giggle to herself. The man was right.

Libby Quinn was making a list. This was the Libby she recognized.

She made a slow walk-through of the bedrooms, the bathrooms, the laundry room, and the pantry.

She spent the day surveying what she could about what it meant to be a steward of this place.

She made lists, plans, and did research on her phone on everything from heating and cooling costs to period details of this turn of the last century lake house.

She needed this distraction, this project. She'd had enough wallowing in the wreckage of the last year.

She went to sleep in her new old home knowing that tomorrow, she had a mission.

And that mission was this house.

* * *

Libby woke up early, took a walk, drank coffee, and was raring to go to town by nine. She would have set out earlier but feared some of the local stores wouldn't be open that soon.

Even in its heyday, downtown Irish Hills didn't get buzzing early, like Chicago or a metropolis. Nothing was a big enough emergency to require flipping an open sign before eight.

In 1989, Irish Hills, Michigan, was the cutest little resort town in the tri-state area. Libby owed meeting her gang of Sandbar Sisters, as they called themselves, to the fact that all of them were here for the summer. Their families owned or rented places along the miles and miles of lakefront.

Except for J.J., she was here year-round.

Libby, Hope, J.J., Goldie, and Viv rode bikes from their various lake cottages to meet up at the gazebo, Dairy Queen, or Tut's. They wore peasant blouses and cutoff jeans. Polyester dresses and beat-up white Keds.

To say that children who grew up in the late 70s and early 80s were feral wouldn't be entirely accurate. Libby's mother was a stickler for manners, properly combed hair, and tucked-in blouses, but she loosened the reins when she didn't have to look at Libby. Or when Libby's presence or politeness wasn't reflecting on her mother.

In the summer, here, in this place, Judith Dana Quinn let the reins of parenthood go entirely.

In part, that was because her mother was only here for one week, while Libby spent the whole summer on Lake Manitou. Libby's mother didn't worry that her fancy friends would see Libby's feral side. They weren't here. Judith Dana Quinn was concerned with events, social status, knowing the right people. This dovetailed nicely for Libby's father. Her father was a city councilman and later a representative to the state legislature. They were busy people, connected to a million causes, and fixtures at all the right charity dinners.

Libby had followed in their footsteps in so many ways. She realized now, though, in the Irish Hills, she ran wild. Maybe her parents knew that was a luxury afforded children, not adults. They knew her well enough to know that she'd soon be walking the same path as they did.

Running wild. Libby laughed at the phrase, and the memories that merely being here continued to conjure. It was the only time she'd done it, the only time she'd really let loose. Her summers here were unbridled.

Unbridled, running wild—none of these words described her adulthood. Was everyone like that?

Her running wild stage was well past. She was closing in on fifty. If she was going to go running, it would be recorded by her Apple Watch, calculated in her daily caloric intake, and mapped out for the exact distance. The joy in it was long gone. It was running tame.

Libby wasn't sentimental or didn't think she was, but here she was, thinking about who she was versus who she'd set out to be.

She was grateful to put that introspection aside. Libby needed to focus on the current task, getting Nora House in shape. Pressing tasks were the best remedy for Libby's crisis of confidence. Getting things done was her wheelhouse, it was where she used to shine.

Maybe she could shine again.

While the town was run down and empty in many places, Libby was happy to see that the local hardware store was still in business, right where it used to be. The brick structure anchored the end of downtown Irish Hills. A yellow and gold Vernors soft drink ad was still emblazoned on the side facing Green Street, headed into town. It proclaimed the drink was mellowed for four years in wood.

Vernor's! Libby hadn't had a Vernors in so long. She'd put that on her grocery list. If being too skinny thanks to the divorce diet was the problem, two scoops of vanilla ice cream with Vernors poured over it was the solution.

It was to be the first stop on her long list.

A bell jingled as the door hit it when she walked into the store with some of her familiar optimism flickering in her eyes. It wasn't a flame, but it was a spark. She was going to all she could to nurture that spark.

Peck's Hardware was well stocked, it appeared, with the things Libby needed.

She grabbed a cart and started down the gardening aisle. The house needed a new hose. She grabbed the largest one she could find. She noted that the store sold house paint. She'd need that too but didn't know what colors quite yet. Libby put a handful of paint samples in the cart to examine later. She needed a new broom, dustpan, and cleaning supplies. She added it all to the cart. She also grabbed a can of WD40 for a few of the squeaky hinges she'd noticed.

When she was satisfied that she had a good start, she walked back to the service desk. A man in jeans and a Peck's Hardware golf shirt approached the counter.

"How can I help you?"

"I've got a lot of projects actually, wondering how I might connect with a contractor or several?"

"I can recommend some, or you can put the job on the board over by the checkout."

Libby didn't think foot traffic here would yield too many takers on the job board, so she opted to ask for some recommendations.

"Screen repair to start, I have counted no less than two-dozen holes, big and small, at the lake house."

"That must mean a lot of windows, so it's a good problem. What house?"

"Nora House, I'm Libby Quinn Malcolm." Libby offered her

hand in greeting and realized she probably needed to ditch Malcolm when she introduced herself. One more change she'd need to get used to.

"Oh, hey! You used to hang around with my sister, J.J."

"Oh my gosh, you're the little brother, Jared?"

"That's me. It's been decades since you've been back here! Wow."

"Uh, yeah, I just took over my aunt's place."

"Well, I didn't believe she'd be able to pull it off." Jared shook his head, impressed with something, but Libby didn't comprehend what.

"Pull what off?"

Jared pursed his lips shut.

"Oh, uh, just your aunt mentioned she had plans for the house and a few other things." His open demeanor suddenly shifted into something that seemed contrived.

"I guess she did then. I'm knee-deep in screen repairs and outboard motors."

"Ha, yes, welcome back. This is great news. You're a big shot community organizer, she said."

"I was, uh, I did community development and neighborhood rehabilitation in Chicago. Used to." Her aunt had bragged about her? That was sweet, she guessed.

"I do screen development and rehabilitation. Give me your number, and I'll come out and see what's what. Sometimes we can fix them on-site. Sometimes I'll have to bring them in here."

"Really? That's perfect."

"No problem. I mean, the least I can do, you're going to have your work cut out with this whole town, don't want you to be worried about the house."

Libby texted Jared her number. She was a little confused by his comment about her work. The house was her work. But she shook it off.

"You need a salon? J.J. is renting a booth across the street.

She'd love to see you. What was it, Sandbar Sisters? You girls were the bomb. You ran this town!"

Libby laughed. A gang of teen girls on ten speeds, quite the crew they were.

"Yes, that was it. Thanks for the help. I'm a little busy today, lots of things to arrange with the house and such. But just text me whenever."

"Great to have you back in town."

"Thank you."

Libby remembered Jared Pawlak as a pudgy little pest, and now he was almost movie-star handsome. And a business owner. He looked like a heartbreaker for sure. Pudding Pawlak, they used to tease him, she was embarrassed to remember. Well, he'd grown out of that nickname, by a mile—better yet, by a few dozen bulging muscles.

She was struck by the amount of time that had passed. And yet when she'd needed help, someone local, who she remembered from the old days, was here, ready to help. It was kind of amazing. And so different from living in a metropolis like Chicago. There it was chain stores and big boxes all the way. She never had the same clerk twice at the big home improvement warehouse.

Libby looked across the street to the salon that Jared had pointed to. It was a bit depressing. The awning was torn. There was a broken neon sign in the window that read *Hairdo or Dye*. Except the 'I' and the 'r' were burnt out, so it really said, *Ha Do or Dye*. Ha, indeed.

This was not the fancy spa situation she was used to.

She hesitated and decided to finish her errands. She needed groceries. Barton's Food Village was next.

That was also the old name she remembered. It was at the other end of the street. Libby packed the car with her hardware purchases and moved her vehicle closer to the grocery.

Libby figured the nearest Kroger or Meijer stores had to be in

Adrian, which was a good half-hour drive. She hoped all she needed would be here, at Barton's Food Village.

She roamed the aisles and filled her cart with staples. She had a few things to put on the grill and realized she'd need charcoal. Before she knew it, the cart was full. She was only buying for herself, but she wanted to be hospitable.

If Jared wanted a snack after working on the screens, or her aunt wanted sandwiches on her next visit, she'd be ready.

At the checkout, an older man ran her items under the scanner. A nametag on his vest read *Ned*. He was staring at her, and then he figured out who she was.

"Well, I'll be."

"Excuse me?"

"You're Libby Quinn, right? A lot older, but I remember that mop of hair hasn't changed much."

Ned, she realized, was Mr. Barton, owner of this place since forever. They'd never called him Ned. How was he still working?

"Ah, yeah, except for the gray roots."

"I've got Miss Clairol in aisle ten."

"Thanks, uh, I heard Hairdo or Dye does good work."

"Shelly did my wife's hair before she passed, yes. Hey, when are you getting started with your plan?"

Libby forgot how small Irish Hills really was. One minute she was buying WD40. The next minute everyone in town wanted to know why.

"I, uh, when I get home today. Maybe after I get these roots done, so they're not so much a conversation piece."

"Your aunt's counting on you, and so are a lot of us."

"Thanks." She had no idea what he was talking about or what to say. They were counting on her? Surely she could repair a few screens, paint some rooms, and generally fix up Nora House. What was the big drama about that?

Libby watched Ned Barton bag her items. She thanked him, and he turned to help the next customer. Libby loaded her stuff into the Jeep. Her two exchanges with locals today were a little weird but nice. She decided she just didn't speak the same small-town language as they did, apparently.

Libby was about to leave downtown and drive back to the lake house but stopped.

She pulled into a parking spot in front of Hairdo or Dye. She tried to see into the place. The window was too dirty to really get a good look.

Maybe J.J. was in there. At one point in her life, J.J. was her sister, or as close to a sister as she would ever have.

There were good memories, but also, there were bad, terrible ones.

Chapter Ten

Libby

1989, the last real summer

J. J. was crying. That was not her normal state. She was fun, sarcastic, the first to joke, not the first to cry.

That was usually Hope. Hope was too sensitive for her own good. Viv was skittish about a heck of a lot. Goldie went with the flow.

But J.J. was tough, the street smart one among them.

And she was crying.

"He hit her in the face, and then he kicked her."

They sat on their spot on the sandbar and just listened.

J.J. was overflowing with anguish.

"Oh my, your mom, your pretty mom," Hope said.

Viv had an arm around J.J. as the girl shook with the retelling.

"She's gonna have to have stitches." J.J. pointed to her own eyebrow.

Jackie Pawlak was a cool mom. She was hipper than the rest of their moms. She wore halter tops, she smoked. And while most of their moms let them run around the lakes in the summer, all of them had annoying rules the rest of the time. Jackie Pawlak never imposed rules on her namesake daughter, Jacqueline Joan, J.J.

"That guy is scary," Viv said.

"He's on drugs, that's for sure," Goldie added.

Libby had no clue what someone on drugs looked like. Drunk, sure—just go to the Lena's Pizza on a Friday night, and you could see that—but drugs she didn't know a thing about.

"That's not the worst of it. She took him back, he said he was sorry, and *she took him back*."

J.J.'s tears turned to anger.

"Maybe she's just scared to kick him out for good," Hope said.

"Yeah, she is scared, I do know that, but still," J.J. replied.

"What about the police?" Libby offered. Surely the police could help and arrest this degenerate.

"My mother won't call 'em. She says it's over, and it was a one-time thing. But this is the third time. I heard his motorcycle and Puddin' and I hid."

"Oh wow, listen, listen to me, Jacqueline Joan Pawlak. Next time you grab Puddin' and just get here. Do you hear me?"

Libby couldn't make sense of why Jackie Pawlak would let this happen. She didn't know about drugs or adult problems. But she did have a place for J.J. She had a place for all of them. They spent most summer nights here anyway.

"Okay...even at night?"

"Night, day, whenever, that house is big enough for a million people."

J.J. nodded. It was no solution. It was no consolation. But the idea that she could grab her brother Puddin' and run to Nora House seemed to give J.J. a little comfort.

They stayed on their sandbar the rest of the day. The pontoon provided shade when needed and a place for their cooler of pops.

Boats floated by. Tubers, skiers, and kayakers waved. They waved back.

The sun browned their skin and streaked their hair.

Libby would open her door to J.J. and Jared all summer if need be.

She didn't want to think about what would happen in the fall. When she wasn't here. Maybe her aunt needed to be involved?

She brushed the worry aside. Fall was a long way off.

* * *

Libby remembered that day, her offer to help J.J. She'd kept that promise.

But still, a lot of water has flowed under the bridge since then.

Libby had remembered more than she'd bargained for. Maybe J.J. wouldn't be so happy to see her. Maybe J.J. remembered more bad times than good from those days.

Libby palmed her key fob and screwed up her confidence. What was she worried about? Rejection?

She walked into Hairdo or Dye Beauty Parlor and looked around. There were four salon chairs, two on each wall.

A woman with a big blonde bouffant—an honest-to-goodness bouffant—greeted her.

"Hi, we take walk-ins, but I'm elbow deep in permanent solution for Lori here."

The aforementioned Lori was caped, and her head was in the process of processing.

"J.J.," called the stylist with the gravity-defying bouffant.

A woman emerged from the back of the salon.

"Is your bunion putting you in a foul mood or something? They heard you all the way in Washtenaw County, Shelly, jeez."

It was J.J. Libby's heart caught in her throat a bit, to see this old friend. This girl, now woman, was so much a part of her youth.

J.J. was petite, had the cutest little shag brunette hairdo, and a mouth on her. She was always the funniest of the bunch, by far, and wasn't afraid to say what was on her mind.

"No, walk-in, I'm assuming she needs her roots done," said Shelly.

Libby put her hand to her hair. Her roots were bad. She got it. They were bad.

"Yeah, I mean, you can see them from the International Space Station apparently," Libby said.

"Don't worry, I can fix you up. Let me see."

Libby walked in further and to the chair J.J. had indicated. While the salon was cramped, in disrepair, and displaying products that looked way past their use-by date, J.J.'s station was neat, clean, and had some of the things Libby's salon back in Chicago used.

"I, uh, J.J...I don't know if you remember me." Libby's voice was uncharacteristically timid. She didn't recognize herself much these days. Did she really expect J.J. to?

J.J. stared at Libby. Their eyes locked, and it was there, the recognition. Wow, J.J. was so adorable, still.

"Oh, my GOSH! Quinn!" J.J. lunged forward and encircled Libby in a hug. Relief flooded Libby, and she felt a tension in her neck that she didn't even know was there dissipate.

"I'm so old now. I figured I look like a grandma."

"Nothing wrong with that, but please, this model figure, and auburn mane, I'd know it anywhere, except you know, in the middle of the day at my work, thirty years later. What the heck?!"

"Yes, well, auburn these days with a big assist."

"You're back, I mean, it's been forever, but here you are. Man, that Emma."

"I am, and I think I'll be here for a bit."

"Oh, wow, I don't even know where to start. Kids, husband, what's up with you?"

"Three kids, all grown, one husband, all ex-ed."

"I'm sorry, on the ex-thing."

"It's okay. I'm just licking my wounds and starting over at my aunt's place. Uh, now my place, I guess."

"That's so great, I mean *so* great. Well, sit down, let me mix up your color, and we can try to catch up."

"Actually, I have groceries in the car. I was just in to make an appointment."

"Not really necessary, since we're not exactly booked, but okay, when do you want to do this?"

"I need it soon if everyone who's mentioned it is to be believed. How about this, why don't you come by the house? I'd love to have a drink. And we can catch up properly. I'll make an appointment for hair now, but we'll hang out right away."

Libby wanted to put herself out there. She'd spent the last few decades as a mom, a wife, a professional woman, but she'd forgotten what it was like to be a friend. She'd missed it. And maybe the one aspect of her life she'd neglected was the one that could save her now. She had asked if this woman would come over and play, was that was how it was done as an adult?

"Tonight?"

"Yeah, why not?" Then she realized J.J. probably was busy. Libby was the unattached one, the empty nester fleeing from scandal, trying to find a new life. "I mean, if you're not busy," she added. J.J. had a life, no doubt.

"You know, I am free. I'm done here at 5:30. How about 6-ish?"

"Yes, perfect! You remember the way?"

"Honey, everyone knows where Nora House is."

"Right, great."

"I'll bring a bottle of wine."

And on impulse, Libby reached out and enveloped J.J. in a hug. Libby wasn't a hugger, and there she was, hugging her old friend.

J.J. hugged her back.

"Honey, I feel the same way about free wine," J.J. said in her ear.

Libby laughed, and she had a hard time not smiling as she got in her car to head back to the lake.

* * *

She had to see a man about a boat, but instead, chickened out and called.

"Hey, K."

"Hey, Q."

The silly code they'd used to say hi came back without Libby even thinking about it. What was it about your first crush? And why did he have to still be handsome? Libby was in the middle of questioning everything about herself, and Keith was still cool and self-assured. Men.

"How's my little boat?"

"It's all fixed up. I just changed your oil, it was old. That was the issue. I gassed ya up. The old boat is all set to tool around Manitou. I mean, you're not going to want to try going more than a few miles an hour in it, but it's safe and seaworthy."

"My water-skiing days are long over. Safe and seaworthy sounds about right."

"Ah, you used to be able to barefoot. I'd pay to see that again."

Libby was good at water skiing but hadn't done it since Alex P. Keaton was a household name. She brushed off the water-skiing challenge and got back to the business at hand.

"So, uh, I need to come get it." For a moment, Libby pondered how she was going to pick the thing up without a ride over to the marina. Keith read her mind.

"Don't worry, I'll get it to you."

"And what do I owe you?"

"Wait, you owe me? I thought this was Aunt Emma's."

"My situation has changed significantly."

"How so?"

"I now own Nora House, and the boat, and the outdated HVAC system."

"Impressive, the situation certainly has changed. Underestimating Aunt Emma is a mistake, it appears."

"Yeah, uh, I did not expect to be in this situation, but here it is. I'm a lady of the lake."

"I'm glad. I hope that means you're sticking around for a while."

"I think so, yes. I've got a lot to do here."

"You don't know the half of it, I suspect."

"What?"

"I'll get your boat to ya, and this one's on me."

"I couldn't."

"I'm like crack. First boat repair is free, then you're hooked."

Was that flirting? Libby did not have even flirting training wheels. No, it couldn't be flirting. Libby was on guard not to look like some old cougar. She wanted a functioning fishing boat, not a boyfriend, for her fiftieth birthday.

"Fine, yes, thank you." She needed to be professional, formal.

"I'll bring it by soon."

Libby tried to come up with a way to get Keith to accept money. She wanted to quiz him on what he meant by not knowing the half of it when it came to Aunt Emma. She wanted to know how his life was. But she needed to be professional, distanced. She was up to her neck in the unknown right now. Keith's life was not something she should be invested in.

"Thank you. Hanging up now, K."

"Hanging up now, Q."

Oops, Libby had slipped into it again, their old language.

Their standard goodbye, back from the days when neither of them wanted to hang up the land line.

Chapter Eleven

Emma

Emma and Patrick waited for her niece in the drive. It was time to lay the cards on the table; well, at least some of the cards.

Emma watched Libby spring from her Jeep like she had a new bounce in her.

Libby looked beautiful, vital, and one hundred percent more herself than the woman who arrived less than a week ago.

"Aunt Emma, I had no idea you were coming. You should have texted me. I'd have hustled back here. I thought our lunch was tomorrow?"

"Yes, but we do have to talk. It's really past time."

"Okay, sure, come on in. Just let me get the cold stuff out of the back."

Emma, Patrick, and Libby headed into the house. Libby deposited her grocery bags in the kitchen.

"You're already making improvements; I can smell the fresh air. This place was getting musty without me airing it out every day," Emma said. It needed this life, this new blood. Emma was right about that. She was hoping she was right about the rest. She had to be.

"Yeah, well, it's been so lovely outside, hard not to take advantage of the breeze. Can I get you something to drink? Coffee, tea, water?"

"No, I can't drink caffeine after lunch, or I'll be up until next week!"

"Okay, uh, just checking up on the place?"

"No, actually. Patrick?"

Patrick handed Libby the executed documents. There was no going back on that part. Patrick had helped her see to that. He was a legal whiz, Emma knew. This place was Libby's, lock, stock, and barrel.

"I used that debit card today, so thank you for that."

"Wonderful. You're settling in."

"Settling? I'm not sure about settling, but I am digging into the project. You know me better than I thought. I love a project."

"Yes, well, about that. The project is a tad bigger than you realize, I think. And you've had a few days to recover from Chicago and that husband unpleasantness. I need you up to speed."

"Yes, I had people tell me today you had a plan, and I was somehow a part of it. But it seemed like they knew something I didn't. Like what is this house built on a gravesite, Poltergeist style?"

Poltergeist? Sometimes she had no idea what young people were talking about. She steeled herself to drop the other shoe on her unsuspecting niece.

"Gravesite, hardly. Young people are so vexing sometimes."

Libby laughed and said she was amused at being called a young person.

"What's your plan, and how have I unwittingly stepped into the middle of it?"

"I am just going to come right out with it."

"Aunt Emma, the time to come right out with it would have been before I signed the deed."

Emma decided to let that point go unchallenged. Emma needed Libby fully committed, unable to say no, and ready to go to battle. She swallowed, stiffened her spine, and spit it out. "You're going to need to stop the mayor from letting this entire town be turned into a highway rest stop."

"Excuse me?"

"Yes, well, had you done more research, you'd have learned that the entire area is on the upswing. Every single lake is seeing house flippers, new renters, skyrocketing property values, and renewed interest like it used to be. We're almost hip, so hip that out-of-town big city slicksters have decided to try to buy our Irish Hills and make it a travel plaza for a huge development of tacky resort condominiums."

"Aunt Emma, *I'm* a big city slickster."

Emma could see that her niece thought she'd lost it. She wasn't quite clear on the seriousness of the situation.

"They want to build resorts up and down our quiet beaches and tear down downtown, pave that all over, aren't you hearing me?"

"Investment can be good news."

"Maybe, except that means tearing down what businesses are still left in Irish Hills. The ones that survived '89. They want to lay tons of paved roads and make us a highway exit with something called a travel plaza. That's the word they use to make a gas station sound fancy. They want to buy up every square inch of the area they can. That's not so good, now, is it?"

"I'm not sure where we're going here."

"I have spent every last dime paying rents, staving off creditors, buying vacant property, whatever I could for all of the businesses that remain in this town."

This started to sink in for Libby.

"Aunt Emma, that's ridiculous. Why would you do that?"

"Because I want to stop these out-of-towners from ruining this place. And it was all I could think of to do to block them."

"You mean to tell me you risked your own financial future to save, what, Barton's Food Village?"

"And the salon, and the hardware store, and a few commercial buildings in the block downtown."

"The main block of downtown Irish Hills?"

Emma nodded. She owned more than she even knew, more than she could afford. She was cleaned out and down to pennies in her bank account. She had enough to live, but barely. Emma didn't say that, though. She could see her niece was distressed.

Libby sank in her chair. And then her niece looked up at Patrick. Fine, let her think Emma was cracking up. She wasn't, but Emma let her niece have a second or two to process.

"How in the world can I do anything to change this? How do I fit in this plan?"

"I told all of them about you, about your skills at community development. You can save Irish Hills. I know it."

"What? I'm trying to be anonymous here, get my life back on track."

"Well, too bad, I need you. The town needs you. You're a born leader, and that is enough moping around doubting yourself."

"Doubting myself? This is a little more than a crisis of confidence. My husband embezzled thousands under my nose, and I was nearly indicted!"

"You trusted the wrong man. That's not a crime. And you're not the first woman to do so."

"Aunt Emma, I still don't know how you expect me to, what, uh, save Irish Hills?"

Emma looked to Patrick. She needed him to share the legal mumbo jumbo now.

Patrick stepped forward and explained, mercifully. Emma was pretty hale, but her niece was tiring her out. Why couldn't people just do what they were supposed to do without faffing and dithering?

"To start, there is a town hearing in a week or so, in front of the mayor and council. Developers have put the proposal before the board and want them to approve a timeline for enacting eminent domain procedures to takeover downtown Irish Hills. Your aunt has expressed her wishes, that it be rejected, but unless we come up with a plan, it'll happen in the name of progress."

"Oh crap," Libby said.

"Crap indeed," Emma added.

"Your aunt has convinced several business owners you can turn things around for them, that you'll help them fight city hall, so to speak."

Emma had learned something of how it worked, but not enough. There were many different ways companies and governments used eminent domain laws to take over land. Sometimes it was to build a factory, others a highway. It was hard to figure out, since rules varied from county to county, state to state. That's why she needed her niece!

"For this kind of thing, typically, local politicians need to see that it is in the best interest of their political and financial futures to stand against the outside interests. If Aunt Emma owns a bunch of vacant property and she's keeping what businesses ARE here afloat, well, it's hard to argue against the deep-pocket investors."

Libby seemed to be formulating a plan in her head already. Emma knew her niece would think like she did, she knew it was in her nature to charge in and help. She might need a push, but she'd do it.

"See, you know best. I knew you would." Emma patted Libby on the hand. Libby had a very strange look in her eye. No matter. It was settled; her niece would need to get to work.

"You lied to me," Libby blurted. "You're my aunt, and you lied."

"Lied? Child, you are in a jam, thanks to your husband. No

money, no home, no job. Quite the predicament in Chicago. And look where you are now!" Emma waved her hands in the air to indicate that grand home that was now Libby's.

"But there are strings attached, ropes, chains!"

"Oh, come now, don't be dramatic. This is your skillset, is it not? Community development. Working with, what's the word, Patrick?"

"Stakeholders," Patrick replied.

"Yes, working with stakeholders to find mutually beneficial outcomes. You're a stakeholder too now, thanks to me. I've assured all the local business owners you are the right woman for this job."

"I'm not saying I am, or can, or even want to. This is nuts."

"Honey, I *need* you to. My finances are tied up in property all over town. I'll be in good shape if we can fight this off and jump-start Irish Hills. I need this investment to turn around if I don't want to switch to an all cat food diet."

"The local business owners would get market value, at least, to sell out. It's hard to compete with that."

"Ha, the market value of downtown Irish Hills is pennies on the dollar right now, dear. You've been downtown. We're quite the fixer-upper."

"You move back in here; you have the house back."

"Too late, it's yours. The whole portfolio is actually boats and stuff. You really did luck out with this place. Think about how fun it will be when your children come here for vacation! You'll all have such fun! Patrick, we need to get going. I have a bridge game." Emma didn't really have a bridge game. What she had were good instincts. She needed her niece to think there was no other way but to help.

"Aunt Emma, you gave me this house under false pretenses."

"Nonsense, dear. I gave you a new life. Don't be too stubborn to see it. I'll get out of your way and let that brilliant mind go to work!" Emma clapped her hands. The debate was over, she hoped.

Emma and Patrick walked out of the house and to her car.

She didn't look back or let Libby continue to argue with her.

This was the soft sell. This was Libby's chance to come to the rescue on her own.

If Libby didn't, well, Emma did have one more card to play. She didn't want to. But she would.

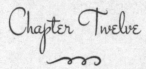

Chapter Twelve

Libby

Aunt Emma was crafty. Libby had to give her that. The old woman had maneuvered Libby exactly where she wanted her to be.

Libby owned this house, and though she didn't have a mortgage, the payments were steep, nonetheless.

She was being asked to save Irish Hills. An entire flipping town!

Libby stood, paralyzed in the same spot. She stared at the empty air where her aunt had just recently outlined this entire scheme.

"Wow. Just wow." Libby said it to no one, into the empty void. *Wow.*

Did everyone know about this plan? What did they all expect from her? This was the opposite of being anonymous. It wasn't licking her wounds and healing. It was feet to the fire pressure from people who Aunt Emma had primed to think Libby was some sort of savior.

She circled the house a few times, pacing, worrying, thinking.

Then sat down at the table in the kitchen. This table was for "the staff," according to Aunt Emma. But Libby loved the vintage Formica-top table with chrome legs. If she stayed, maybe she'd select an office space in one of the rooms, but she loved this space in the kitchen for now. She was the only staff.

Libby flipped open her laptop.

The internet was slow, thanks to an ancient modem, and she'd already called the cable company to come to shore up the WIFI. If she was going to rent this place as an Airbnb someday, she'd need better connectivity. But for now, she had enough bandwidth to do a bit of Googling.

What was the situation here in Irish Hills? Was Aunt Emma exaggerating? Libby got a very serious vibe from the attorney, Patrick. He didn't seem prone to hyperbole, but who knows. Maybe they were all nuttier than a Snickers bar.

Libby knew how eminent domain worked. She'd fought it before, several times, in her work to save old neighborhoods and historic districts. She'd come up against big developers who wanted to bulldoze everything.

She needed to know exactly where Irish Hills was in the process, who was behind trying to demolish the town, and when the actual deadlines were. Her fingers flew across the keyboard. She saved links to articles. She looked up Lenawee County records. She realized she needed a printer.

After all her research, she learned she had exactly one week until the first hurdle was cleared. An outfit called Stirling Development was behind the push, they owned places called Stirling Resorts, and they were a huge company. She flipped through pictures of their luxury resorts from Vegas to Dubai.

The city council and mayor needed to approve a timetable from Stirling, and then Irish Hills would be quickly, easily, absorbed. Emma would have to sell too. She'd have no choice if the plan got the green light.

The question before city officials: Should they proceed with the developer's proposed timeline for assessing value on the property in downtown Irish Hills?

Elected officials would be voting soon to decide if the developers could appraise and make offers. It would be a tacit agreement that locals were on board with the developer's plan.

They wanted to do this by the end of this summer!

Libby sat back and then put her head in her hands. What was her aunt thinking? This was insane.

Libby knew she had the tendency to want to fix things. To charge in and take charge. And look at where it had got her. Broke, divorced, and on the outside of the community she'd tried to build.

Her aunt was wrong. There was no way Libby could fix this on short notice and in the middle of doubting her entire life's work.

Next week someone would have to go in front of the city council and explain why they should reject the timeline.

That didn't stop the project, but it would put the brakes on things and slow it down.

Maybe slow it down enough to buy time for Libby to figure something out.

Libby checked herself. She had mentally just put herself in the role her aunt was trying to force her to take. She saw herself as the one who would argue to slow down the developer. No. No way.

Oh brother.

A low rumble pulled her from her personal pity party and laptop screen.

Libby stood up and went to the back window. There was a familiar boat with a familiar captain chugging toward her dock.

Keith.

Libby experienced brief regret that she'd not taken J.J. up on the immediate hair appointment. Her mop was still rooted in gray. It betrayed the years.

Libby indulged herself in a quick look in the hall mirror. There was some mascara under her eyes, smudged, no doubt as she melted down over her current conundrum.

She rubbed off the worst of it.

"Oh, heck with it," she mumbled. This man was here for her boat, not her.

Libby jogged down to the dock. Keith slowly brought the boat alongside it, and Libby remembered how to tie it like she'd been doing it every day since she'd left. Funny what you keep and what you don't.

"Expert level," Keith said.

"A skill I didn't think I needed."

"You very much need it, now that you're the Lady of the Lake."

"Ugh, I think I might actually be the biggest sucker of the county, turns out."

Keith jumped off the boat and onto the old dock. "How so?"

"Ugh, nothing. My aunt, she's a lot more devious than I thought."

"Oh, she's sharp as a tack, as they say, no doubt."

"Yeah, tack is right. I stepped on the point."

"Ouch."

Libby looked up at Keith. At 5'7", she thought of herself as tall. When she wore heels, she was the same height as Henry. Keith had been a lanky teenager. They were the same height when they'd met, and then he'd shot up and left her in the dust. He was over six feet and had filled out nicely since she knew him.

Libby told herself this was a dispassionate assessment of her old friend, not her checking him out.

"So, the motor, really, what do I owe you?"

"Nada, like I said."

"Well, can I offer you something to drink? Wine, water, pop? I'm recently stocked."

"If you have a light beer, I'd say we were more than square. But only if you're joining me."

"I could use a glass of wine, for sure. Make yourself at home. I'll go get it."

Libby dropped her worries about hair, clothes, and the rest of it. She found that the idea of sitting on the porch and catching up with Keith was the distraction she needed. Her problems were there, sure, but she wasn't helping herself, spiraling out of control at the mercy of her manic Google searching.

She found Keith arranging the old Adirondack chairs on the back porch.

"Here, optimal viewing," Keith said. She handed him a beer.

"Sorry, hope these hold us. They're ancient."

"They're in good shape. Coat a paint maybe," Keith said.

"You're right. A lot of paint is needed all over this place."

"It's still grand. It's only been the last decade or so that your aunt let stuff slide."

"She's something, alright. But enough about me, and my old aunt and old house. How are you?"

"Me, well, as good as the Lord and my wife will—" He stopped mid-sentence.

"What?"

"It was a corny thing I used to say when I wasn't a widower."

"I like corny. So, how did you meet?" She wanted to know about Keith. She was tired of being in her own head about her own problems. She hated it in fact.

Libby also hated that she had no idea what had happened in Keith's life.

She'd left here in a hurry and never looked back. She'd run away. She saw that now. After she'd betrayed his trust. She'd acted like a really dumb teenage girl. Thanks to that, this person she used to know so well was a stranger.

"I met Carrie when I was at basic in Parris Island. She was a South Carolina girl. For some miraculous reason, she waited for me when I was traipsing all over Iraq."

"How long were you in the military?"

"I was in until I retired, about ten years now. Bought this place from Steve after I started getting that pension. Carrie had decades of putting up with my deployments. Raising the boys on her own a lot of the time. We moved here to settle, you know? If I'd have seen the future, we would have done it sooner."

Libby could see regret and pain etched in the lines of Keith's face.

"You loved her a lot, that's clear. I'm sure she knew that."

"I did my best, but it couldn't chase away ovarian cancer."

Libby winced. She knew the truth of that, her mother-in-law had fought it years ago now, but she understood. It broke your body and heart in increments until it took everything.

"It's as cruel as it gets."

"Yes, that it is. Didn't mean to bring you down. We're doing okay, the lads and me."

"That's what we moms want to know, from here, or from Heaven, that you're okay. And that you'll get a haircut now and again."

Keith laughed, and the sadness evaporated. He took a swig from the cold beer Libby had provided. She'd find out his brand and stock it for the next time. The next time?

"That's the Q I remember, bossy as heck."

"Yes, true. I own it."

Keith knew too well who Libby had wound up with. He didn't have to imagine Henry. Henry's family also had a summer place here. Though he was older than Libby and her friends.

"So, Henry and you, three kids, you said?"

"Yes, great kids. Not so great of a marriage, you hit the jackpot there, while I wound up with snake eyes, let's just say."

Libby knew that love was not etched on her face when she recalled her marriage to Henry.

"I heard he is, uh, on the lam."

"Yeah, he drained our finances and dragged my name through the mud before he left. So, here I am, trying not to be a burden on my kids. And trying to figure out what's next."

"Well, I'm not going to say I told you so."

"But you told me so," Libby finished the thought.

One, two, princes kneel before you. She didn't know it was a turning point all those years ago, but it was.

"I know for a fact that whatever you do, you do well. Whatever is next."

"Thank you."

They sat together, she sipped her wine, he drank his beer, and the sun glowed bright orange as it fell behind the trees over the lake.

"Wow."

"I know, easy to forget how spectacular it is until you come on back."

They didn't have to talk, that was the same as before. And when they did talk, they didn't have to explain. It touched Libby somewhere in her chest, maybe even her heart, to feel that connection with Keith. Was the young woman who knew Keith much different than the middle-aged one of today? She felt a little joy thinking maybe they weren't so different.

"Hey! Hello! Did you start without me?"

J.J. stomped around the porch and found them both. She had a bottle of wine at the ready as well.

"Well, look at here. It could be 1988 all over again," J.J. said. "You two in deep conversation, drinking before I had a chance to."

"J.J.! Pull up a chair, the best show in the state's about to go down," Keith said and indicated their sunset view.

"Man, this place is stunning. Still." J.J. looked around the house.

"Yeah, hopefully, it's not an albatross ready to drag me down. Well, further down."

J.J. sat down in the chair Keith had arranged.

"Oh, your aunt, she dropped the bomb on you, eh?" J.J. said.

"You knew?" Libby looked from J.J. to Keith. "What about you?" He nodded sheepishly.

"Okay, spill it. You're both natives. I have a lot of questions."

Chapter Thirteen

Libby

"She's been paying people's rent, she says, and her lawyer confirms she's spent most of her considerable savings on keeping this town afloat by buying the vacant properties. Has she paid yours?"

Libby was laser-focused on her two friends. It was a blunt question and none of her business in normal circumstances. But she needed answers since she was being asked to bail out her aunt and this town.

Maybe they could help her figure out how to handle her current predicament. At the very least, they knew more about today's Irish Hills than she did.

"Me, no. I bought Steve's Marina outright, debt-free in my case. But she's helped the grocery store, Peck's Hardware, right, J.J.? And she's been tap dancing to keep 'em all in business."

"What about you?" Libby looked at J.J.

"Nope, I don't own Hairdo or Dye. I rent a booth. Honestly, that place is a wreck, no offense to Shelly, but if I had a salon, it wouldn't be, uh, well, you saw it."

"Sure, but do you know if Shelly needed help? And if Aunt Emma gave it?"

"Yes, on both."

"So, she's bailing people out. Great. But the ship here is sinking anyway. I don't have to tell you both that Irish Hills looks...well, it looks like that tornado came through yesterday."

"That was the end of the heyday, for sure. We're a waystation to the lakes and ripe for the plucking," Keith said.

When he put it like that, it was obvious why developers were circling and hoping to take over.

"There are a lot of great business owners here. The problem is nothing has been updated since the first Bush Administration," J.J. explained. "Lake houses are popping up all over the entire chain of lakes. My husband Dean is a contractor, and he's busy as heck, but still, there are adorable little hamlets all over now."

"The way I heard it, the suits from Stirling Development looked around and thought, which hamlet could be bulldozed with the least resistance? And Irish Hills was the easy winner," Keith said.

"Winner at being a loser, story of my life," J.J. said.

Libby looked at J.J. and wondered about the comment. There were so many things she wanted to know, to catch up on. They'd lived a whole life without each other and the rest of their Sandbar Sisters. Once, they'd known every detail about each other. And Libby was feeling a lot like a loser lately, too. She understood it. She just didn't want this point on her life's journey to define it.

"Please, you're always too hard on yourself," Keith said and gave J.J. a gentle push on the shoulder. They were still friends. A little pang of envy surprised Libby. She steered the conversation back to the problem at hand.

"I do know a thing or two about rallying a community behind an idea and then, well, working with city hall to get it done. That was my life in Chicago. Before the thing imploded."

"Well, it sounds like your aunt is a genius then, not an evil mastermind," Keith said.

"The jury is still out on that," Libby replied. Her aunt had maneuvered her with the skill of a master chess player. Libby had to decide if she wanted to play or cash in and run.

"Look, I, for one, love her plan to get you on our side. Let me help you. We need something here. If we don't want to be a rest stop on the way to better places," J.J. said.

It gave Libby a warm glow to know her old friend believed in her after so many years. She didn't want to let J.J. down, much less her aunt or Keith.

"I guess I could try, dig in a little, talk to the business owners."

"Right, yes," J.J. said.

She caught a smile on Keith's face, too. So maybe he didn't want her to run off either.

There was no reason these two people should be so sweet and loyal to her. She'd been gone for decades. But they were, and their support, even more than the push from Aunt Emma, did the convincing.

"Okay, I'll look into it. I'm not promising anything, but you two have convinced me not to pack up my suitcase and drive out of here as fast as my Jeep will take me."

"Well, we'll take credit, but it's probably also that view," Keith noted, and they all sat for a moment and watched the sun sink behind the horizon.

A golden glow lit the lake. There was a hint of the recent early spring thaw. Things were still soaked with the memory of snow. But it was May now and unseasonably warm. It was a tease for the summer. May in Irish Hills was the time of year that the summer renters didn't see.

Shame that, Libby thought.

Keith was right, if there was a more beautiful spot on earth, Libby didn't know it.

But did she have the skills to do what they needed here?

She took a sip of wine and hoped for the best.

The three of them wound up talking and sipping for several hours. Libby laughed, reminisced, and felt more at home with Keith and J.J. than she'd felt in years.

The problem of saving the entire town was still in the back of her mind. But at least, thanks to her old friends, she had a better sense of it and two allies who'd stood the test of time.

* * *

Her first stop the next day was to J.J.'s booth at Hairdo or Dye.

"Girl, that was the most fun I've had in a while. And it's the first time I've seen Keith really smile since Carrie."

J.J. massaged the shampoo into Libby's hair. It was so long overdue.

Shelly wasn't at the salon yet, but she was another item on the list for Libby to check off.

A little more research this morning had proved fruitful, and Libby had a better handle on the situation.

The hearing next week was preliminary. If Libby could get more time, show the local politicians that there was a benefit to saying no to the plans to turn the town into a rest stop, well, maybe she could find a way to turn the town's economic fortunes around. Maybe she could somehow make Irish Hills the hub it once was.

"I'm going to trim the ends a bit too. You need a refreshing."

Libby trusted J.J. She always had.

As J.J. worked, Libby felt a wave of regret, guilt even. They'd all scattered and left J.J. with barely another word after that tornado. But here she was, no malice or anger. She picked up with Libby as if it was 1985, and they were trying to figure out a ride to the mall on a rainy day.

Libby came out with it and said what was on her mind.

"Did you hate me, hate all of us, for losing touch?"

J.J. paused a moment and switched focus from the foils she was putting into Libby's hair to her eyes in the mirror. "No, not one bit. I know we all did what we had to do. And well, it worked out."

Libby didn't push too hard on that comment. Had it?

"How is your mom?"

"You know, she's a pain in my keister, lives with me and Dean part-time."

"Oh, wow, that's a full house?"

"Now that the kids are out, it's less so. And mom spends winters in Florida. It's just that she'll be back soon, and ugh. Dean helps me stay patient. But she still smokes, she still has a knack for finding deadbeat boyfriends, and she still insists on having a Harvey Wallbanger after dinner every night."

Libby laughed at the thought.

The image of J.J.'s mom, bruised, vulnerable, and so pretty back then, popped into Libby's memory.

"We did the right thing," J.J. repeated. "It's all good. And I know your aunt was devious to get you back here, but I'm glad she did. I was fresh out of old friends."

"Me too," Libby said.

"Now, let's get the dowdy out of your hair."

Libby didn't pry anymore. She wondered why J.J. didn't have her own salon, or what her kids were doing, or how her relationship was with Dean. She'd never met Dean, but there was affection in her voice, not bitterness when J.J. mentioned her husband.

It made Libby happy. Maybe some couples did get a happily ever after.

J.J. gave her a blowout and swung the chair around to face the mirror.

"You do great work!"

"I do, yes, and you are looking ten years younger, if I do say so myself. Remember that time that guy was hitting on you because he took you for the girl in the White Snake video?"

"Ha, yeah, I wish I looked like Tawny Kitaen."

"Well, the closest match in Lenawee County! And God Rest Her Soul." Libby had been very flattered back then when she was mistaken for Tawny Kitaen. It made her surprisingly sad when she learned the actress had passed away. Another bit of their childhood gone.

Libby's Tawny Kitaen red hair was back, thanks to J.J. Libby still had the crows' feet and the bad attitude, but she had to admit her hair was an improvement.

"I can't believe some big salon hasn't snapped you up."

"Story for another day."

Shelly arrived, and Libby decided to practice her pitch with J.J. there as backup.

"Shelly, I have a question. Just wondering, how are you feeling about this possibility of the town being bulldozed and turned into a travel plaza?"

"Me, well, it wouldn't be the first time we've been leveled, eh?"

"Yeah, 1989, mother nature did the job," J.J. agreed.

"But are you managing here?" Libby pressed. "What would it take for you to want to stay?"

"Honey, J.J. here is all sunshine and roses. I know the facts. The facts are that the other towns around here have tourists with the big bucks. I'd like to stay if I could make this work. But a buyout? I'm not going to lie. I'd look at the offer."

"But if, say, I could help get more foot traffic here, in Irish Hills, get more of the tourism dollar, what then?"

"Yeah, maybe. I wouldn't say no to good income, but would it be better than selling out?"

"That would be my aim."

Libby wondered if she'd find the same attitude with the other business owners. Were they ready to fight to save the town? Or were they beat down enough to accept a quick payout.

J.J. walked her out to her Jeep.

"That doesn't sound too encouraging," Libby said.

"Don't worry about Shelly. Even if you had a million people walk through here, she's not up to the latest styles or methods. Half of my clientele comes to me after Shelly tells them the best plan is to set their hair in curlers and do a bouffant."

"Okay, so where next?"

"Talk to my brother, at the hardware store, talk to the grocery. The old golf club might be good, too."

"Yeah, they'll be more receptive?"

"I know my brother wants to stay, and Ned Barton, too; they want to make it work here. They just don't know how to compete. No one comes here. Why would they?"

"Got it."

"Also, I cleared my calendar. I'll be your wingman."

"Really?"

"Well, not really. I didn't have any other bookings but you. It's dire around here."

"Okay, well, let's get after it then."

They took a quick walk to Peck's hardware and found Libby's brother Jared.

"Oh, oops, you need me to check the screens!" he said on seeing Libby. "I promise I'll get to you!"

"Nice work, slacking for your possible big-ticket customer." J.J. punched her brother in the shoulder.

"Hey, I got behind. The stock boy called off yesterday. Today, too. Can we catch ya later this week?"

"Whenever, it's not mosquito season quite yet! But that's not why I'm here. I have another favor to ask."

"Ask away," Jared said.

"What would it take, from your perspective, to survive here, without this so-called plan to turn the town over and let developers transform it into a travel plaza?"

"I need to compete. I need foot traffic. The place needs to be like it was before. Or I'll be hitting your aunt up until that well runs dry. A lot of us will."

"Why don't they come here, in your estimation?"

"Easy, there's a big box in Adrian, and ugh, the downtown looks rundown as heck. No foodie level restaurants, no microbrewery, all those things draw people from the cottages and into town in the summer."

"Got it. What do you offer over Home Depot?"

"My sexy smile, is that a thing?"

"No, it is not, you're gross," J.J. said.

"Seriously, customer service and I know every inch of the electric and plumbing in the older cottages. Nothing's standard if you catch my drift. Look, I don't have everything under the sun here, but I do have what you need when you're spending the summer sunning, get it?"

"I get it. If I was to fight city hall on this, if I could buy time before they make a decision, would you back me?"

"I'm sure I would. My sister might beat me up if I didn't."

"Yep, got that right," J.J. said.

Jared rolled his eyes at her.

"Great," Libby said.

"But I'm really not enough," Jared said.

"Sexy smile and all," Libby quipped.

"Don't encourage him," J.J. interjected.

"I've got a few more stops to make. I need to have a small army with me by next week," Libby said.

"See, she's bossy, but it comes in handy," J.J. said.

"No wonder you two were BFFs, bosses of a feather, boss together," Jared joked.

"Is that the saying?" J.J. said with a raised eyebrow.

Libby smiled, watching them interact. She hoped her own kids had this kind of bond. But truth be told, all three were scattered across the country. It made her heart hurt a little. Seeing how J.J. and Jared were there for each other made her think her kids could be that way in tough times, too.

But on to the problem in front of her. She had Jared and Shelly on her side, more or less. It was time to recruit other business owners to push city officials to keep Irish Hills, Irish Hills.

She made great progress at the grocery store, the used car lot, and the propane tank filling station. All of them were mainstays from the old days, and all had pinned their hopes on Emma coming through with the rent, as she had been. And they believed Emma's promise that she was finding someone to stand up to the developers.

If Libby could convince the politicians to delay this, maybe they would be on board for rehabbing the town. Though that was one worry too far right now. Libby just needed enough support to buy time.

It was a good day, a long day, but she felt a little hope when she got home.

Libby realized she hadn't eaten much between her hair appointment and taking the temperature of the beleaguered small business owners.

She opened the fridge. She'd spent decades worried about feeding the kids, or Henry, and having enough, and making sure it was healthy and on and on.

It was still new, dinner for one. It was weird that no one else's daily schedule impacted hers.

Libby decided she liked not worrying about the food pyramid or dance practice or figuring out what to serve if Henry's new client showed up. Nope. That was all over.

No matter what happened here with this half-baked scheme of her aunt's, she did not, at this moment, need to worry about dinner.

Libby scanned the shelves; she knew this kitchen needed an upgrade. The harvest gold appliances were so old they were back in style again, but they did the job.

She pulled out the cream cheese and schmeared it onto a bagel. That's right, a bagel, for dinner, with no guilt.

She took her meal, such as it was, out to the back porch. It was a little chilly, but Keith had been right. This view was everything. Libby would enjoy it while it lasted.

She'd thought she'd have a lot of time to chill. She'd come here to figure herself out. Decide what came next. She had come to Irish Hills for space to breath.

But Aunt Emma had moved into that space, and so had the fate of the town.

J.J. and Keith, they were back in her life now, too. How in the world?

She counted herself lucky at that.

Libby looked out to the water. Golden sparks from the setting sun danced on the surface. The birds were just waking up to the new season.

Maybe she was too.

1988, Nora House

"Did you kiss?"

Libby flushed red at J.J.'s question.

"Give her a break. Of course, she did. Keith's a super fox," Hope said, coming to her rescue. As much as Libby was the one in charge, in most things, Hope was the one who knew boys.

Hope had dated scads of them back her Ohio hometown. Hope broke hearts everywhere she went. Hope was the flirt, the expert.

"Irish Hill's answer to Johnny Castle," Goldie said. Marjorie Gould fashioned herself as Baby Houseman when she came to the lake. As such, she also insisted on a cooler name than Marjorie. Goldie was the best they could do since Baby didn't work for the oldest of the Gould kids.

They'd all seen *Dirty Dancing* a million times, but Goldie was the actress among them and quickest to compare everyone to a movie star or a *People Magazine* cover.

Libby rolled her eyes, but Goldie was right. Keith Brady wasn't a dancer, he was a local, but he was just as cute as Patrick Swayze. He was also just the kind of boy that her parents would be annoyed with if they were ever here at the lake. He worked at the marina, filling up boats, fixing them, doing whatever his boss said needed doing.

Luckily, her parents were rarely at the lake, so they had no idea how serious she'd gotten about Keith Brady.

"So, how did he do it? Like while they were playing 'Hungry Eyes'? Please say it was while they were playing 'Hungry Eyes'."

Viv, as the youngest, had exactly zero boy experience. While Hope was the Zsa Zsa Gabor of Cedar Point Road, Viv was Tatum O'Neal in *Bad News Bears*. Two years difference in age but a lifetime of boy information.

Her friends continued to push her for particulars. Every summer, they danced their hearts out at the Red, White, and Blast Bash. It was a huge event on July 4th weekend. They'd always gone as pals, but this year, Libby had a date.

Keith, who'd been her buddy, her lake best friend almost as much as the girls, had turned the tables on her and asked her on a real date.

If you'd asked her any summer up to that summer, if she had a crush on Keith, she'd have said no. Libby would have protested like it was an outrage. Keith was her friend; he wasn't boyfriend material. But she protested too much, as they say. She'd had a crush on Keith from the moment they met. The chronology for her crushes went Davy Jones, Shaun Cassidy, John Stamos, and then Keith.

But Keith was real. And he'd had the guts to ask her to the Red, White, and Blast Bash. When he did, he'd moved from the make-believe *Teen Beat* impossible column to the real-life actual date column.

He'd driven her to The Dance Pavilion. The old venue housed

roller skating most of the summer, thanks to Libby, but this event was a no roller skate date. Keith had opened the car door for her, and he'd held her hand. She wanted to say it was weird, going from friends to boyfriend and girlfriend. But it wasn't. It was right. It was the way Libby had wanted it all along.

She decided to throw a bone to J.J.

Libby braced herself for the squealing that would scare the feathers off the swans currently gliding by the dock.

"Yes, we did kiss. Not on the dance floor, but at the car, before we drove back."

The squealing commenced, as expected.

Libby answered all their questions. There were a million questions.

And they stayed out on the dock until well past one in the morning.

Libby didn't tell them that after Keith kissed her, she'd glanced up at the sky, with her head on his shoulder, his arms tight around her waist. She watched in awe as a star streaked across.

She kept that detail to herself because it seemed made up. But it was real, and Libby knew she would never forget it.

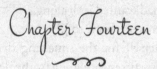

Chapter Fourteen

Libby

Libby had a full day planned; she'd get to every business she could. Since Irish Hills was small and, in many ways, like a ghost town, it shouldn't be too difficult to find out where the majority of locals stood.

Then she'd visit the mayor's office and be sure she was on the agenda for the meeting.

The local golf club was the first on the schedule. She'd called yesterday, set an appointment to meet the owner.

There were half a dozen golf courses in the area. Irish Hills Country Club was the nicest. If any of the businesses would want to stave off big developers, maybe it was the club? After all, a big resort might be competition.

They had a rich history and a beautiful location. There were a million ways this venue could help bring in people and customers. Libby's mind was abuzz with possibilities.

She drove up and remembered long-ago dinners here. Boring dinners. Dinners where her parents insisted she dress up. Dressing up in the summer was the worst thing a young Libby could think of.

She'd rather run around with her girl gang and then, of course, Keith. Libby blushed, just like she had all those years ago when her teenage crush came to mind.

Keith miraculously was her friend again. He'd lived a life with the love of his life, and it wasn't Libby. Enough time had passed that she should be able to look back fondly and move forward as friends. Her brain knew that, but her hormones were set to 1989.

J.J. and Keith made this current mission more personal. Almost as much as her aunt's predicament, it was her friends that had motivated her to give it her all.

The winding drive of the country club ended at the top of a hill; the old clubhouse loomed. It also needed paint, new gutters, and a million little things to turn into something high-ticket weekend renters would pay for.

It was in her nature, she knew, to try to fix everything, to take on projects, to take charge. Each place she visited since yesterday sparked a million ideas about how Irish Hills could move forward. Rehabbing and rescuing were in her blood. She usually found a way to spark new life in old spaces.

It was a curse in a way, and the path that led her to where she had been in Chicago. She really should leave well enough alone. This was her aunt's doing, though. Her aunt knew Libby couldn't say no. She was in it now. Libby let her instincts to fix and manage off the leash. She'd need every one of them to pull this off in the time she had.

Libby had decided to look as corporate as she could for this meeting. She'd kept two pairs of tailored slacks, one black and one tan, and half a dozen crisp solid-colored blouses. And she'd saved her navy-blue blazer. It was prudent to have one or two suits of armor, she reasoned. Libby was glad to have them now. It made her feel like her old career-woman self.

Libby also adorned herself with the tasteful gold jewelry. The kind her mother raised her to wear. It was the most buttoned-up she'd been since she'd gotten here, but she felt like it was in order.

The Irish Hills Country Club used to be the place for tasteful vacation preppy attire, so Libby knew she'd fit right in today. She had memories here, too, of her parents fixing her up on a date with Henry. She remembered how badly it went when Keith had found out.

She'd disappointed Keith by trying not to disappoint her parents. If they'd lived to see how Henry turned out, maybe they'd have laid off and let her date who she'd wanted to.

Memories she'd not dwelled on in years flooded through her mind from the moment she walked in.

Mother's and Father's Day brunches were here. One of the obligations of getting to do what she wanted in the summers was to sit through those brunches.

She could smell the waffles, the omelets, the bacon, the syrup, as though it was soaked into the wallpaper.

She remembered them as something to get through, so she could ditch the white puffy-sleeved blouse her mother liked and get back to her friends.

Libby was older now than her mother had been when they'd had those brunches. She brushed off that thought. Time had moved so fast from that moment to now. This place made her miss her seventies chic mother.

Libby looked into the empty main dining room and could almost see Judith Dana Quinn, spectacular scarf, gold hoop earrings, and bright red nails, picking at her food. But thoroughly enjoying a Virginia Slim cigarette.

There were ghosts in these rooms, Libby realized. She shook them off and focused on the task of the day.

Libby knew where the offices were and headed that way.

The door to the office suites was open. She strode in. There was no secretary, so she moved from the reception area to the main office. A man wearing a green golf shirt sat at the desk. The Irish Hills logo was embroidered with white stitching on the side.

He was younger than she was, she decided. His face and arms were already tanned as if it were the middle of the summer. A feat in May, but probably the byproduct of working at a golf club. Libby suspected Clyde Brubaker had a classic farmer's tan. However, she did not want proof of this assumption.

"Mr. Brubaker, Libby Quinn." Libby thrust out her hand for the handshake. The rest of the world might be doing elbow greetings, but here, in Michigan, old ideas died hard. He stood and shook her hand.

"Quinn, ah yes, fine family."

Clyde Brubaker had never met her, but the names Libby and the Quinn were synonymous with the early days of the area. First, the auto barons like her ancestors built the fancy big houses, and then their executives flooded in to build all the cottages. The Libbys, Fords, Dodges, Fishers built or rented summer homes on the area lakes. Clyde Brubaker knew the history, it appeared. If not for the Libbys, there wouldn't be an Irish Hills Golf Club.

"Ah, thank you."

She wasn't here to deflate his obvious pomposity; she was here to get the man on her side.

"Before we continue, let me loop in my investor." Clyde punched a few buttons on his phone. "Mr. Stirling? Yes, Libby Quinn is in my office, and you're on speakerphone."

"Good morning, Ms. Quinn. I'm in meetings in Manhattan and couldn't make it in today." The man's voice was deep, with a hint of a New York accent. Libby sat up straighter, this was as different ball game than she'd prepared for. Mr. Stirling? Stone Stirling was the CEO of Stirling Development.

"I realize I didn't give much notice before wanting to meet, and I didn't realize the club had outside investment partners." Libby's language reflected the new information that was now filling in the blanks to an entirely different scenario than she'd envisioned.

"Ah, yes, closed the deal. What, last week, Clyde?"

"Yes, we're so fortunate to have a partner like Stirling Development."

Libby was searching her brain like it was Google trying to get a fix on what she knew about Stirling Development. This meeting had shifted up a gear. It wasn't her brainstorming with a local business owner to delay the mayor. It was something more serious and corporate all of a sudden. She felt unprepared, but here she was. She'd been in big meetings before, so she pushed ahead.

"I'm here to talk to you about the plan to use eminent domain to destroy downtown Irish Hills and turn it into a travel plaza. I've spoken to several other business owners in town, and there's quite a bit of opposition to the idea."

"Yes, Clyde let me know that you'd talked to a handful and have set meetings with several more. You work fast."

"Well, it's just that the meeting is next week, the mayor and council will decide to move forward or take more time to consider. I'm of the position that taking more time is the way to go."

"Oh, really, more time for the town to whither, for businesses to go into debt? That seems counter-productive to everyone's interests." The voice on the phone wasn't forgiving, wasn't interested in compromise, and was clearly irritated by Libby's initial foray into stopping eminent domain proceedings.

"Actually, everyone I talked to likes the idea of more time." The luxury of more time had been afforded to them by Aunt Emma's retirement accounts, but Libby didn't bring that detail up.

Clyde Brubaker smiled in Libby's direction, or maybe it was a sneer. She was feeling a lot less welcome here than she had during her mom-and-pop shop tour yesterday in town.

"Let us make things perfectly clear and save you any further embarrassment and time. In addition to investing in this property, the country club, to turn it into a world-class golf course, we're also in full favor of maximizing the potential of the region, that means construction of luxury resorts, improvements of highways, bolstering infrastructure, and—"

"Bulldozing downtown Irish Hills so you can have an easy-on easy-off travel plaza. That's obscene."

"Calling it downtown is generous. Debt, ill repair, and complete lack of vision is what the analysis I read clearly shows. Despite being in the heart of a gorgeous region of untapped resort potential."

"Untapped? We love our cottages and lakes."

Libby felt like he was attacking one of her kids. And a fierce protective streak rose up in her. An out-of-town development corporation had decided they were going to make money here, and local business owners and residents be damned!

"Clyde, can you let Ms. Malcolm know where we stand, officially, and why she'll stand down immediately. I've got to get to my next call. Good day."

The line went dead. The debate, as far as Stone Stirling was concerned, was over.

Libby did an internal double-check to ensure her mouth wasn't hanging open. What a pompous jerk! He'd clearly never been here and was deciding the fate of Irish Hills based on spreadsheets.

"So, where we stand, officially, clearly, is in favor of Stirling Development Corporation's visionary plan to remake the region into a resort mecca."

"Clyde, condos, big hotels, a new highway loop—all of that will kill everything that's amazing about living on these lakes."

"It is very clear you have a love for the region, which brings me to the part about why you'll stand down."

Clyde put a manilla file folder in front of Libby. She reluctantly opened it.

Inside the folder, she found a tidy stack of articles, with the headlines that haunted her nightmares, still.

Non-Profit Funds Missing
    Charity CEO Accused of Cooking Books
    Citizen of the Year Facing Indictment
    Gambling and Graft Mark End of Marriage and Reign of
Chicago Super Couple
    Libby Quinn Malcolm Steps Down Amid Scandal

Libby swallowed hard. She also blinked away tears. For a few days, she'd forgotten how hard these headlines had smacked her down. She'd believed in her ability to make a change, to help.

It was a harsh reality she'd glossed over in an attempt to be who her aunt wanted. Libby wanted to cry, but she wouldn't do that in front of this toady for Stirling Development.

"This is old news, Clyde. I was cleared. My ex-husband is the bad actor here. My record is clean."

"Well, funny, isn't it? None of that really made the front page, did it?"

The man was right. And it was why she was here, not back in Chicago, moving and shaking and rebuilding her life. The fact that she wasn't indicted didn't get the big splash in the papers or on the news. Everyone in the state of Illinois attached the name of Libby Quinn Malcolm to a financial scandal.

While the locals didn't seem to hold it against her, she had come here with her tail between her legs. Stone Stirling knew it. It wasn't hard to find dirt on Libby, and the minute she stood in opposition to Stirling Development's plans, Stone Stirling got his shovel and started digging.

Libby stood up. She didn't want to break down in this office.

She didn't want this stranger to have the satisfaction of seeing her lose it.

"Thank you for your time." That was all she could muster. Libby turned and walked out. Behind her, she could hear Clyde Brubaker laughing. He was actually laughing!

What a jerk!

* * *

When the oily muck of bad feelings, doubt, and regret ooze into your heart, it opens a fissure for more of the same to seep in. It takes but a few jagged breaths for your lungs to fill and drown out all the positive self-talk, the manifestation of goals, the live-your-best-life mantra you repeat in an effort to make it so.

Libby drove back down the long drive of the golf club. She didn't see the buds on the trees. She didn't see the cottages in the distance or the sparkle of the water between roof lines.

She saw her mistakes, writ large.

She remembered one, maybe her first irreversible one, at this very country club. She let Henry kiss her, even though she knew her heart was Keith's.

That's what had played out the last time she was here.

1989, Irish Hills Country Club

Henry had asked her to dance in front of her parents. There was no way out of it without getting "the look."

So, they danced, one fast one and one slow one, and then Henry gave her a huge break. Maybe because he was in college? He was more worldly, more aware of how to get them both out of this situation.

"Okay, you have satisfied the 'rentals. Want to 'Walk Like an Egyptian' onto the porch?"

"Yes, please."

Libby felt a flash of guilt that Henry could see she did not want to dance with him. She had been doing this for the 'rentals, the parentals, her parents.

Henry found a spot on the bench that overlooked the golf course. The ninth green was in close proximity. Libby could have sat across from him, but she didn't. She sat down next to Henry Malcolm.

He produced a cold Bartles & Jaymes wine cooler and tipped it toward Libby.

"Here, we can share."

"Thank you for your support," Libby said.

"What, oh, I just knew you didn't want to dance anymore, been there myself."

Libby had been referencing the commercials for Bartles & Jaymes. Her joke fell flat, and she felt stupid. She didn't speak college guy.

Henry handed her the glass bottle, and she took a sip. He reclined on the bench like he owned it, and his arm draped casually around the back, behind Libby. She noticed but tried not to react. Libby never worried about being cool, yet for some reason, with Henry, she felt the need to seem older and nonchalant. Though, as her friends teased, she was the most 'chalant' person they knew.

Drinking was a new experience for Libby, and even one sip gave her a fuzzy feeling in her head.

"When are you headed back to Ann Arbor?"

"Next week. I'm living in the frat house this year, so none of that freshman dorm room bull."

"Ah, sure."

Libby had forgotten the name of Henry's fraternity. She was too embarrassed to ask again. If she was older, she'd know, and she'd also know the cool nickname for it. To cover, she took another sip of the wine cooler.

Libby had her senior year of high school to manage, then college. She was ninety percent sure she was headed to Northwestern. Joining a sorority was well down the list of things to worry about in Libby's near future. Though Henry didn't ask.

"It's hard to remember that you're not in college yet." Henry shook his head, looked her up and down, and whistled quietly. There was something dangerous in the look.

"Thanks."

"You grew up a lot this summer, I can tell."

Libby felt Henry's palm on her shoulder, and he pulled her closer as he angled himself in front of her on the bench.

And then he leaned in and kissed her. It wasn't tentative, or sweet, or something they'd waited to do for years and years. It was the opposite of how she and Keith had circled around the idea before they finally crossed the lines of friendship.

"Wow," Henry said as he leaned back and leveled a look at her again.

Libby was proud of herself for a second. She'd kissed her second boy and didn't suck at it. It wasn't Keith. It was different, not terrible. But it confirmed for her that Keith had cornered the market in terms of butterflies and all that.

"Libby."

Libby's heart dropped to her stomach.

She knew the voice before she'd seen his face.

The sugary remnants of the wine cooler felt thick and coated her tongue.

Keith, he was there, and he had seen her with Henry.

Keith's face told all she needed to know about his reaction.

* * *

Keith had sweetly come to see if she needed a ride after the stupid dance. And he'd seen her.

Henry had been nice, she remembered. He was patient. He drove her back to Nora House and didn't try to kiss her again. He was making choices then, too, she realized. He was deciding to invest in Libby and not dismiss her distress about her 'townie' fling, as he had jokingly called it.

Libby leaned on Henry then, and it had started a trust between them, even as Libby freaked out about Keith.

She didn't blame Henry; she'd made her choices. She'd broken Keith's heart of her own volition.

Keith was her first. And back then, in 1989, they were young enough to believe they were old enough to talk about forever.

The breakup devastated Libby, so much that even her parents noticed. They said no one knows what they want at seventeen. She let that idea in. At almost fifty, she now agreed. They were all right. But still, maybe her heart did know more than her head back then.

She remembered the guilt. She remembered exactly how she felt, hurting Keith to satisfy her teenage curiosity. It was a decision that changed the path of her life. Teenagers make turns that seem small, but in hindsight, you can see that each one puts your feet on a different path. Sometimes it is a small change, of course. Other times, like her kiss with Henry, it was a 180-degree shift of direction.

Libby remembered how much she'd hurt Keith. She remembered those raw emotions now that she was back here, at the scene of her crime of the heart.

Libby had let Keith go without a fight. How could she know, at seventeen, that one kiss was really a life choice?

She only saw Keith one more time, after that. And then he pulled up in the boat last week and hauled her middled-aged self to the marina.

The porch of the stupid country club was a moment in time in her life she'd tried not to dwell on. Yet here she was again. Clyde

Brubaker had purposely taken her down. Little did he know her biggest regret wasn't from a few months ago, it was from decades ago, and it had gone down right here.

This was too much. She'd come here to get away. The idea was to regroup, not fight with big developers, or try to rescue the town. Instead, she was subjecting herself to a powerful millionaire CEO playing hardball.

She needed to get her own act together. She needed to lick her wounds, not expose them to strangers with buckets of salt.

She didn't care what her aunt wanted her to do. She couldn't. Libby was damaged goods when it came to community organizing, much less saving this town from the likes of an international development company.

Libby knew what she needed to do. She turned the Jeep North on Green and East on Twelve.

She'd made her decision. Her aunt wouldn't like it, but that was too bad.

Chapter Fifteen

Emma

"Dear, this is unexpected! Come in, come in."

Her niece was rattled. That much was obvious.

Emma asked Libby to have a seat on the davenport.

"Davenport? You still call it the davenport?"

"A large sofa that converts into a bed, yes, what else would be more apt?"

Emma walked into the kitchen and put a teapot on the stove. Her niece was clearly working up to something. Emma decided to move slowly, deliberately, and let her niece get to it in her own time.

Emma watched Libby pace, run her fingers through that enviable mop of hair, and she seemed to be struggling to stay glued together, despite something inside of her pulling her apart.

"Aunt Emma, I can't do it. I understand why you set me up for this, why you thought I could, but I can't."

"Do you want sugar or even honey? I love a little dollop of honey in my tea."

"Aunt Emma, listen. I tried. I really did. There is just no way anyone is going to trust me to lead a community effort with my past, my reputation."

"Oh, nonsense." Emma stayed calm. Maybe her niece would calm herself. Though it did not look likely.

"I thought maybe you were right, maybe I could help. I thought maybe no one knew about what happened with Henry or that they'd see it wasn't my fault, but I was lying to myself."

"Who put the bee in your bonnet on this?"

The last Emma had heard, her plans to get Libby's considerable leadership skills working for Irish Hills was going along swimmingly. Emma had felt relieved that she didn't have to enact her more sinister method of getting Libby's help. Except now maybe she would.

"Bee in my bonnet? Aunt Emma, you're kidding, right? This is more than a bee in my bonnet. I have a swarm of murder hornets trapped in my sports bra. That's where I am right now."

"I do not have the foggiest idea what that means."

"It means I can't do what you want me to do. Call Patrick. I'll sign the house back to you. You can sell it. Or I'll sell it and give you the cash. You won't be destitute. You can still live here with the proceeds."

Emma let her niece continue to prattle on about her plans for quitting the fight. It was useless to try to get a word in while she spiraled.

Emma sipped her tea.

"Dear, that's just not acceptable. The house is yours, and I'm not taking it back. Also, those corporate suits will buy, no doubt, but they'll tear it down. They have no interest in the history, remember?"

"Look, I know you're used to getting your way, but you can't force me to stay here. I'm not the person you think I am."

Emma knew exactly what kind of person Libby was. She was the kind to get the job done, she was indefatigable, she was smart, confident, a good mother, and a great friend. She'd just forgotten that, thanks to a bad patch with a lousy husband. Emma had no choice; it was time to apply more pressure to her niece.

"I think it's the opposite. I know exactly what kind of person you are. That's why you're here."

"Aunt Emma—"

Emma put up her hand. She didn't have the lung capacity to get into a verbal sparring match with someone half her age.

Libby stopped talking and stopped pacing.

Did her niece sense the shift in tone the conversation was about to take?

"I know your secret," Emma said. For a moment, her niece looked confused.

It was a long-ago moment, in the midst of a cyclone.

But Emma had seen what happened. She knew what the girls had done. And she may go to hell for it, but now she was going to use it. Their secret was Emma's trump card.

"What?"

"Not so ready to blow your wig now, eh? I saw you and your friends turn him away."

"Blow your wig? Uh, Aunt Emma, are you sure you know what century we're in?"

"I do, and I saw you and your Sandbar Sisters. I know you locked the door. I know that man was out in the cyclone, blown to Sunday like Dorothy Gale, probably."

Libby squared her shoulders and locked eyes with her aunt. "So, you saw? You were there?"

Aha, there it was, an admission.

"Well, it wasn't easy. Things were chaotic. The devil's dustbin was swirling around Lake Manitou. But my eyes were good back then. And I was there."

"What are you getting at now? What does that have to do with anything?"

"What if I remembered what happened, what I saw, to someone other than you?"

"Are you blackmailing me?"

"I would never do such a thing."

"That night, we were protecting someone. It wasn't like you seem to think it was."

"I don't think a thing." Emma gave her niece the most innocent blink she could muster.

"But you're implying that you're going to, what, call the authorities, about something that you think you saw in 1989, in the midst of a tornado that leveled most of the town? I thought you might be out of touch with reality. Maybe I was right."

Ooh, her niece was feisty. That was the feisty she wanted. It was the fight the town needed.

Emma decided to let her niece know she was not batty, confused, or experiencing bouts of dementia. What she was doing was protecting this town, using every tool she could think of.

"I have noticed that it does not appear the papers are very keen on depicting you in a favorable light." She let that sink in with Libby.

In a million years, Emma would never do a thing to hurt her niece. But her niece needed a push. Emma was pushy from the get-go. It was a genetic trait that came straight from Nora Sullivan herself.

Emma knew pushy was just another derogatory term for women who took charge. Just like the b-word. Today's b-word was yesterday's 'pushy' or 'forward,' as her mother was called. They were always coming up with words to knock down a woman with confidence. Emma owned pushy, just like Libby owned bossy. Sticks and stones, as they say.

Libby was angry. Emma saw it. But she was also a woman with a truly good heart. She didn't point both barrels at an old lady. Emma had banked on that too. Being ninety had very few advantages; however, it was still uncouth to attack a nonagenarian. In this case her age would be her shield not her weakness.

Libby lowered her voice, lowered her anger at her dear old aunt. Emma knew she would. She also hoped her niece didn't look too far into the leverage Emma was using.

"Aunt Emma, I could still do everything I can think of and lose. Are you going to ruin me if I can't save this place?"

Emma wasn't going to ruin her niece, not by a long stretch, but her niece didn't need to know that yet. If she let Libby off the hook, the woman would run, wallow in her recent troubles, and be no use to anyone. But Emma did soften her stance. She loved Libby and hated kicking her while she was down. She was trying to kick her into gear!

"You're due for a win. I have no doubt that those wins will happen right here, in Irish Hills."

Libby plopped herself down on the davenport, finally! All that pacing was tiring Emma out! Libby was shaking her head in disbelief, smoothing her eyebrows, and generally letting her body cycle through escape options even as her head realized there weren't any.

Libby looked up at her. Oh, her niece was a beauty. Libby's eyes were the rarest of the rare. A light green, like Emma's mother. The hair, too, was a distinct call back to Nora Sullivan.

Beautiful Nora, a maid, an immigrant's daughter, had caught the eyes of a young auto baron.

Her father once refused to talk to her mother for an entire month after Nora Sullivan Libby had cut her auburn hair. They were a pair, those two.

Looking at Libby now, Emma remembered her parents like she'd seen them yesterday. That wasn't always true, it was hard to remember sometimes. But Libby, with her Irish up, brought the face her own dear ma back to life, like the last sixty years had vanished. Libby had generations of strength to tap into.

Emma could see that her niece was tired, too self-deprecating, and unsure of this new middle-aged phase of her life. Emma knew

Libby was just getting started. If the younger woman could re-imagine, like all women must do after a certain age, she'd rise like the auburn phoenix she was! Emma could see it clearly. Placing this challenge in front of Libby would help her niece rise again.

All of that remained unsaid. She'd let Libby find her way, with the big push Emma had just delivered.

Libby fixed those cat eyes on Emma. The uncertainty had faded. Libby had wrestled with the situation but was now stealing herself to face it.

Ha, Emma had her. She knew it.

"So, I'm going to do it. I have no choice. I get that. You've outplayed me, old lady. But I need you to promise that you'll never breathe a word of what you saw that night to anyone."

"I'll take it to my grave. I expect that grave to be in the Irish Hills Memorial Cemetery on the outskirts of a thriving town. Thanks to you."

"Fine, fine."

"Oh, good!" Emma clasped her niece's hands in hers. She might have temporarily wounded her with that little boxing round. But now Libby knew the stakes! Her niece was in this fight to the end. No more dithering or doubt.

Chapter Sixteen

Libby

Libby left her aunt with a promise to do all she could and with the knowledge that now, one more person knew what they'd done that last summer they were together.

It was one of those days that imprinted on her memory. A lot of the summers were a beautiful amalgamation of sensations. But that day was singular. And vivid.

And not just for Libby, for anyone who was there when the tornado came through.

But it was a more personal storm that rushed forward to great the Sandbar Sisters. And her aunt knew.

1989, Nora House

J.J. came running to them. Out of breath, her bike crashed onto the grass next to the house. J.J. always carefully employed the kickstand. Only an emergency would allow her to treat her wheels so carelessly.

The rest of them were standing on the dock, gawking at the weird sky.

"Batten down the munchkins," Goldie said.

"No kidding. Dorothy," said Hope.

The wind was starting to pick up, and the sky was yellow on top and black down low.

Libby turned to look at J.J., who was gasping for breath.

"Man, were you biking against the wind?" Viv asked J.J.

"No, no, it's Bruce."

"What?"

"Mom's boyfriend, Bruce, I threw a lawn jart at his head, and, and—"

J.J. had tears in her eyes. She tried to explain but struggled for breath and words at the same time.

"Did you hit him?" Libby asked.

"I did. I mean, he swore like I did. He was holding his eyebrow like I broke the skin. He'll probably need stitches."

J.J. had hurt her mother's boyfriend, Bruce. As far as Libby was concerned, that was well deserved. But J.J. had more to tell.

"He's chasing me. He is coming after me. I'm telling you I need to hide."

Libby looked around the side of the house. No one was there.

She put a hand on J.J.'s shoulder. The little thing was shaking.

"We know he's a bucket of ralph, but did you have to throw a lawn jart at his head?" Hope asked.

"Yes, he came after Jared. My mother finally grew a spine and pushed Jared into the Gremlin. They drove off, but he was trying to stop them. I clocked him with the jart and pedaled the heck out of there."

"Good for you. Your mom and Jared are okay?" Libby asked.

"I think so. They didn't stop to see what had happened. They just drove."

Libby imagined the scene.

"You're like Wonder Woman. I mean, you saved your mom," Libby said.

"Yeah, well, I biked fast, came right here, but he knows I hang out here."

"You came to the right place. We'll kick him in the family jewels if he tries anything," Hope said.

"I think we're going to have to back that up. Look," Goldie replied. She pointed to the long drive that ended at Nora House. In the distance, they saw him.

"He's walking like Freddy Kruger or Michael Meyers. We're screwed," Viv said.

"No, no, we're not. Let's get in the house. We can lock the doors."

Libby was yelling now; the wind was roared too. And then they heard more than wind, a howl came from Bruce. He was yelling something about J.J. It was impossible to understand the exact words, but easy to understand that he was enraged at their friend.

The girls ran from the dock to the back porch.

"Get in, get in, get in!" Libby slammed the back porch door and engaged the bolt.

"What's happening?" Goldie wondered.

A siren now joined the roar of the wind. The wind seemed almost like it was hungry, like it was chewing the oxygen around them but couldn't get enough.

"I'm sure he's still out there," J.J. said. She'd run to the front door.

"We need to get in your basement," Hope said.

Libby's brain darted between the weather bearing down on them and the enraged man coming up the driveway.

"Yep, I know, I know."

Libby ran to the front door. She didn't know where her aunt was, and her parents wouldn't be here until the weekend. There were no other adults to make any decisions. They were on their own with a tornado on one side of them and a violent man on the other. Libby engaged the bolt on the front door, too.

"All the other doors are locked tight." Viv and Goldie had run around the house, making sure.

There was a crash from somewhere upstairs. There were open windows, but it was too late to worry about that.

Libby looked out the window that faced the driveway. A tree limb ripped loose from the old willow and smacked the glass. She'd just had her face right next to it! It could easily have shattered into her cheeks, her eyes.

All the tree limbs in the yard were bent over, distorted. It looked like they were in pain from the wind.

"Oh, oh my goodness." Viv was at the back of the house now.

They all looked. The huge wall of windows faced the lake.

It gave them a horrifying and panoramic view.

A black swirl on the other side of the lake edged toward the water. It jumped and jerked. Its randomness made it all the more terrifying. And it was huge. It had already blotted out the sky with its inky smudge.

"He's on the driveway."

J.J. wasn't looking at the storm. She was focused on the man outside. Bruce struggled against the elements to get to them. Was that the level of rage J.J. had incited in the guy?

What would he do if he was trapped inside with them instead of out?

Libby looked at J.J. and made the decision.

"Hope is right, the cellar door is there. Let's go, that tornado is going to lift the house off the ground with us in it!"

Viv, Goldie, and Hope ran to the cellar door and scrambled down the steps. J.J. stopped, and the girls looked at each other. They heard him yell. His voice broke through the sounds of the wind outside.

"Let me in you—" The rest of his commands, his bellows,

were swallowed up by the howl of the cyclone. The house was yelling too. They heard floorboards crack and pop.

"Go," Libby said, and J.J. nodded. J.J. ran down the steps. Libby took the first step. She grabbed for the cellar door. It flapped out of her fingers.

It was as if all the air in the house was being pulled out, away from the center.

There was no more doubt or debate. Libby ran down the steps. She missed a few and fell the last couple to the bottom. She landed in a pile of her friends.

The electricity flashed and then went out.

It was oddly quiet for a split second, and they heard pounding on the door. Was that Bruce? Or was it a branch hitting the door?

Cacophony. A word so infrequently used but apt for this moment. Libby remembered it from her college prep tests. It popped into her head just then. Cacophony.

The lights flickered again, and they were in the cellar, in the near dark. The roar intensified so that no voices, no pounding, nothing but the wind filled their ears and sucked the air from their lungs.

The tornado was there, over them, around them.

They held hands, huddled together, and prayed it didn't sweep them all away.

Many in the path of that twister did not survive it.

Certainly, Bruce hadn't.

* * *

Driving through Irish Hills today, you could still see what the Cyclone of '89 had wrought.

Ultimately, the twister had skipped over Nora House, but it did not miss downtown Irish Hills. It flitted over Main Street, randomly sparing and destroying.

It took Lincoln Dry Cleaners. It ripped through St. Joe's Catholic Church.

Thankfully, it was summer because the small elementary school in Irish Hills was leveled. Had school been in session...unthinkable.

Libby felt such sadness now, to know that none of the places had been rebuilt. The Catholic Diocese in Detroit decided against fixing St. Joe's. If they didn't see the upside of restoring Irish Hills, how were the small businesses going to do it?

Even the deep pockets of the area, the auto executives were out of cash. GM had idled factories, Ford closed plants, and layoffs were common. Rebuilding in that climate wasn't feasible.

Libby didn't have to summon the memories. The Cyclone of '89 had carved chunks out of Irish Hills that could still be seen today. It had accelerated the decline of the little town. No matter how hard the local business owners tried, they were fighting uphill.

Libby had blocked Bruce out of her memories. She'd deliberately pushed out the guilt, the fear, the images of an enraged man trying to get to them. He fought the wind to try to hurt them.

She'd locked what they'd done away in her mind, just as definitively as she'd clicked that bolt shut to protect her friends.

They'd all talked about it, worried about what happened to Bruce. But after a few days, in the wake of the destruction of the town, their concerns about a man they couldn't see were replaced by the wreckage they could.

Bruce wasn't from Irish Hills. He was one of many of J.J.'s mom's boyfriends. No one seemed to be missing him.

Libby had stopped worrying about it, had put it out of her mind for decades. The man was violent and abusive, and they were girls.

They'd all made a pact not to talk about it. They'd emerged from the cellar of Nora House and agreed. It was almost as if it didn't happen.

But it did, the Sandbar Sisters all knew. They'd locked the door on Bruce. And they'd locked that moment away, all of them.

But Aunt Emma knew too, and she'd made no such pact. She was using that moment to get her way.

Ugh. Crafty old thing.

Libby picked up her phone and dialed.

"Libs, what's up?"

"I need to talk to you. You free?"

"Sure, come on over to the house. I'm just doing some laundry. Dean is getting ready to go out."

J.J. had lived in the same house her whole life, the one her mother had. Libby was expecting to find the same look, but as she drove up, she realized the place had been totally redone, likely between J.J.'s husband, Dean and her brother, Jared.

There was new siding, an L-shaped addition on the side, and gorgeous landscaping. All of it made Libby realize how much time had passed.

J.J.'s house was two streets over from Green and Manitou Lake Road. There were only a few clusters of neighborhoods inland at Irish Hills, and this was one.

Libby noticed many of the houses looked fixed up. It surprised her. She parked and walked up the front sidewalk. Before she could ring the bell, a burly man opened the door.

"Hello! I'm Dean, J.J.'s husband! She'll be right out."

"Nice to meet you."

"I've heard a lot about you, one of the famous Sandbar Sisters!"

Dean was almost too big for the little house. His head wanted to scrape the ceiling, and his burly width certainly couldn't have made it through the front door without angling sideways.

His baritone voice was warm and welcoming.

"I don't know about famous, though one of us is, actually." Goldie had done exactly what she'd set out to do back then.

"Well, Lenawee County famous, how about that?"

"I'll take it."

"J.J., get your sweet ass out here!"

A laugh escaped Libby's throat.

"Oh, nice, I'm in there folding your four-hundred-pound jeans, and you're out here being crass with the company." J.J. emerged from a door at the end of the cozy kitchen.

"The house is amazing," Libby said.

"Thank you, love, this one knows a thing or two about construction." J.J. kissed her husband on the cheek.

It was about as wholesome a thing Libby had witnessed in as long as she could remember. She realized that her own marriage had ended horribly, but it was bad from almost the get-go. She and Henry never had a sweet connection like these two.

"I do what she says, or I gets the hose," Dean said.

The size difference was hilarious between them, and the fact that Dean bowed down to J.J. as the boss made Libby smile.

"Well, you both have turned it into a lovely home, though I miss that orange shag carpet." The place had also mercifully lost the smell of Virginia Slims Menthols that hung in the air around Jackie Pawlak.

"Don't worry, when mom comes back in the summer, she rolls out every bit of tacky she can find, so she feels at home."

"Well, I'll let you ladies catch up," Dean said. "I've got some deck stairs to build for a new owner out on Cedar Point Beach."

"Is that an all-day thing?" J.J. asked.

"Yep, and I'm headed over to the VFW tonight. If you need dinner, that's where I'll be. Meeting Keith and them."

Keith and them. Libby surmised Dean must hang out with the group of men from Lenawee County who'd served from WWII to Afghanistan. Dean must be a vet, too.

There was something so purely small town about it, though she knew those groups existed in Chicago. It seemed to be more of a thing here.

"Got it, thanks."

The burly bear of a man patted his little wife on the head. She swatted him away, but for her trouble, she was pulled into a hug by her hubs.

"Love you."

"Love you, too."

This was the dream. These two were the kind of marriage people wanted.

"I mean, he's adorable," Libby told her friend once Dean had left.

"Yeah, these days, sure is. We've had our moments, but the last ten years or so, well, it's been the payoff."

"That's wonderful. I'm envious. Henry and I never had that."

"You're not dead yet," J.J. quipped.

"Ha, yeah, well, speaking of the dead." Libby winced at her own transition.

"Your aunt okay?"

"Oh, yes, she'll live forever, and she's far from dead. I think we might want to sit down for this next bit."

"I've got coffee on, here, have a seat. I'll pour us some."

Libby didn't mind the delay. She had to say something she'd been avoiding talking about for thirty years.

She looked around the kitchen. It was beautiful, really. Simple taupe shaker style cabinets, a clean soapstone countertop, and sweet pictures of J.J. and her kids on the walls. The girls appeared to be the spitting image of J.J. and her boy, a burly bear in training. Libby hoped she could stay in J.J.'s life, that she could learn about what the kids were doing. How they were getting on.

She felt sick again that she'd let this part of her life go by the wayside. But her aunt's threat reminded her why, in part at least, she'd fled from Irish Hills and hadn't looked back.

"So, spill it, you look kind of green."

"I tried to pull out of this 'save the town' fantasy my aunt has. Some big players want it turned into a rest stop."

"Yeah, this I knew. That's why your aunt called in the big guns, you!"

"Yeah, but they play rough, these big companies. I'm not sure if I can hang with them. So, well, anyway, I have to now. I went over to my aunt's because I was going to bow out, and she brought up Bruce."

J.J. rocked back in the kitchen chair. She shook her head. "That piece of crap, wow. Had you thought about him lately?"

"No, I'd sort of shoved that into the denial file."

"Ha, yeah, exactly. What did your aunt say? How could she possibly know?"

"Aunt Emma said she was there, at the house. We didn't know it. I mean, I thought it was just us. But she saw what we did and implied she was ready to share it with everyone if I backed out."

"Whoa. Stone cold."

"Yeah. I mean, I don't even want to say this out loud." Libby looked around the house to be sure they were alone.

"Oh, I know, I know."

"But did we kill that man?"

J.J. sucked in a breath between her teeth. Libby let the worst question in her life hang in the air over the kitchen table.

She put her coffee cup on the table but kept her fingers entwined in it. She leaned forward, and the two women locked eyes.

"He beat up my mother, was hitting Jared when mom ran, and well, I don't even want to know what he planned for me."

"He was an awful excuse for a human."

"And he was coming for us, he was."

"Yes, I rehashed it in my mind on the way over. But I locked the door, we all hid, we let him stay out there in the tornado."

"We have no real idea what happened to him. Eight people from Irish Hills died that day. There was chaos, tragedy," J.J. said.

"He wasn't a part of the eight they found," Libby said.

"Right, he was a cockroach. I like to think he skittered out of town."

"But what if the wind swept him into another county or a lake or—"

"That's what I've always pictured. What do you want to do?"

"I don't know. Do we go to the authorities now?"

"And say what, that thirty years ago during an F-5 tornado five girls hid in the basement while a drifter walked up the driveway?"

"My aunt says she saw. She must have seen him pound on the door."

"Look, your aunt said she's going to what, blab if you don't help her?"

"Yeah."

"And you were going to fight Stirling Development anyway— well, you were, before you got intimidated by the big boys."

"I'm not intimidated by the big boys." Libby bristled at the characterization. She'd had a major job before Henry knocked the wind out of her sails. Big boys hadn't scared her before, much.

"That's the Libby I knew. Now you've got several reasons to fight for Irish Hills."

Libby bit the inside of her cheek, an old tic that re-emerged in uncertainty.

J.J. pressed on. "You're doing it for all of us, the business owners that are still here, trying to make a go of it, and you're doing it because your aunt is going to wind up destitute. She's been so generous to the people here. They're rooting for her and you."

"Yeah, but then Aunt Emma just handed me the worst motivation ever," Libby said.

"What's that?"

"Fear."

Libby had a very real fear that her aunt wasn't bluffing. Aunt Emma could open a can of worms that the press who already hated Libby would love. That would ruin Libby and maybe her friends.

"Honey, I think you've got it backward. Fear is the best motivator."

Libby cocked her head at her friend.

"Think about it," J.J continued. "The only reason I don't eat chocolate for every meal is that I'm afraid of diabetes."

Libby laughed. It felt good. She'd been wound tight by Aunt Emma and Stone Stirling's threats.

"Okay, so I shouldn't warn the old gang that we're about to be outed as murderesses?"

"No, no, it's all okay. Just do your thing fighting those developers. Focus on that."

"There it is, back to the main issue. I have to find a way to make it worth the mayor's while to delay this thing. That's the first step."

"Any idea on how to do that?"

"All the businesses say they need hope, traffic, a way to bring in customers."

"So, what's the plan? Can you do that?"

"I have no idea."

"Well, I have no fear. You'll figure it out."

"I thought you just said fear was a good motivator?"

"Don't listen to me. I haven't had chocolate yet today. I'm delirious."

Chapter Seventeen

Libby

It was going to be a warm day. As the month of May took hold, the weather seemed to be seducing Libby. June and July were gorgeous here, that was no doubt. But during April and May, the weather could be a roll of the dice in the Great Lakes region. Chicago was no different in that regard.

Spring had decided to show Libby what summer could be.

The sun was warm, and the weatherman declared with glee that the day would see temperatures in the upper seventies.

Libby was thrilled to feel the morning sun beam in through every window. It helped her hope that she could do what lay ahead.

Libby's emotions were all over the place. She was determined to help with one breath, and on the next exhale, she felt the need to run from her aunt and this responsibility.

She was up early and walked the whole house. She decided to open the door to the attic at the end of the second-floor hallway on a lark. She climbed up the steps to the massive space.

It was filled with effluvia. If Libby didn't have a million other things to do, she'd love to spend more time up here. She walked carefully among stacked boxes, old dressers, and a baby carriage. A sunbeam illuminated the dust particles her footsteps had stirred.

She'd gotten rid of her stuff, Marie Kondo-ed the heck out of it. And here, in this house that she now owned, was century's worth of new old stuff. Libby didn't have the urge to get rid of a single thing. What she wanted to do was sit in this attic and leisurely pick through whatever caught her fancy.

But she didn't have time. She scanned the huge space that ran the length of Nora House. Maybe someday.

A stack of boxes caught her eye, and then a sneeze exploded from her.

Whoa, the surprise attack sneeze meant it was a peeze, and that meant she'd need to go change. The indignities of being of age!

The box at her shoulder level was labeled with a strip of masking tape. The writing on the tape was faded, but Libby did make out the years 1930-45. Libby was curious and decided to grab the dusty thing and take it down with her. She didn't have time to paw through the attic, but maybe one box would be a fun distraction some evening.

Libby was a dusty mess after descending from the attic with the old box. She showered, poured a cup of coffee, and took her cup out to the back porch.

Her old friends had been right about sitting by the lake, it was medicine.

Those old friends were counting on her, but she didn't know if she should be counted on.

Just a few months ago, the only way to save her life's work was to fall on her sword and leave it.

That was the last taste in her mouth when it came to her efforts as a community development leader.

Back then, she was in a no-win situation, and here she was again. Except there was no stepping down. Her aunt had maneuvered her quite well. It turned out her escape hatch was a trap.

Libby walked into the kitchen. Documents were spread out all over the table. She read and re-read the plans that Stirling Development had filed at city hall. They laid out a slick plan to convince the mayor and three council members to turn over Irish Hills.

Stirling Development knew there was massive potential here. They'd mapped out the fifty lakes. They'd noted that NASCAR had just completed renovations on the nearby Michigan International Speedway. They pointed out that miles and miles of beachfront were under-developed and ripe for luxury condos. Stirling Development outlined how the dilapidated Irish Hills was just a sore thumb and could be the key to making the area a tourism mecca.

Libby was angry. Stirling Development was right. This area was a gem, undiscovered by most. But did Irish Hills have to be wiped out to make way for the good times these proposals predicted? The business owners who'd stayed for decades were struggling. That struggle made them an easy target. Libby wanted to help them find success, not push them out of the way so others could.

But was that her, just agreeing with her aunt because she had to?

She thought hard about it. Would a huge resort be so terrible? What if it was better for everyone to sell out to Stirling? What if the area could be the next Lake Tahoe or Branson? Those places were amazing. Maybe the best thing that could happen to the small business owners was a tidy little buy-out.

Her aunt would just have to sell.

She started to research market value. And that's where she could see why her aunt was desperate. Except for Keith's marina, every Irish Hills business was struggling at best, underwater at worst. Stirling Development would be able to pay pennies on the dollar for most of it. They'd buy the Tut's building, the grocery store, and almost anything they wanted for next to nothing.

If Libby had time, she knew she could turn things around. The entirety of the Irish Hills commercial district was smaller than the Chicago neighborhood she'd poured her career into. She'd helped increase affordable housing there, encouraged neighborhood events, and matched local merchants with small business loans. But that had taken decades. This hearing was less than five days away!

Festivals, events, and art fairs were ways Irish Hills could lure people to the town. If they could make this a lovely place for the lake renters and vacationers to visit, well, they'd have something. She could envision luring vendors, sponsors, and pitching travel journalists. But not in five days.

On May 9th, she'd need to convince the mayor to hold off on the eminent domain, or at least delay the timetable that Stirling wanted to impose. For that, she'd need to show the mayor that the residents were against this development plan. Further, she'd need some sort of alternative.

Just saying no was a weak strategy. She needed a plan.

Her aunt could blab to anyone who would listen about Bruce. Her aunt's threat wasn't going to magically give Libby an idea on how to fix Irish Hills. Libby was going to fail. This town was going to go under, her aunt too, not because she didn't try, but because there just wasn't time.

She reread the proposal for what seemed like the one-hundredth time:

"Irish Hills is perfectly situated to provide convenient accommodations for the modern traveler. But the town, as it stands, is in disrepair. Inspections of several buildings indicate they should be condemned. There are no viable restaurants or even gas stations with modern fueling requirements. Construction of an access road from what is currently Manitou Lake Road that leads to Green would be an essential piece of longer-term development efforts. The proposed resort area around Lake Manitou and the rest of the lakes would require fuel, food, and modern amenities. The proposed service plaza location is positioned for easy highway access and convenient travel for visitors. Refer to Attachment 4."

Attachment 4 was a rendering of an amped-up highway exit and sterile travel plaza.

The proposal continued to harp on the dilapidated Arrow Gas Station, run by Arrow Orwig. Poor guy, another one who'd only survived lately because of Aunt Emma. And one who had no way to upgrade to fight Stirling Development. Arrow would come out and pump your gas, but if you wanted to plug in your electric vehicle? Or, to get E85, you'd best move on to Ann Arbor.

Ugh, Libby felt like she was trying to pull a rabbit out of a hat. Every avenue seemed like a dead end. She read and reread the proposal.

She did sense the local business owners wanted to stay, to fight, but that they had no idea how. And they were tired. Thirty years of fighting for survival will do that to you.

She banged her head on the table.

"Hey, Q, what did those brain cells ever do to you?"

Keith was on her porch. Somehow, she'd missed the sound of his boat motoring to her dock. She'd been treading water in the deep end of her self-doubt.

Keith looked like he was ready for a day on the boat.

"Hey, K. Do to me? More like for me. And nothing, it turns out. Absolutely nothing."

"Can't be that bad," Keith said.

"Yeah, well, if I don't come up with something, the town is going to be a travel plaza. So it is that bad."

"Ah, so the weight of the entire world is on your shoulders. That's your favorite thing, I remember now."

"It is not my favorite thing. I didn't have a choice. It was my aunt. She foisted this on me under the guise of a lakeside retreat."

"Seems to me you've already done this before."

"You mean in Chicago? Yeah, sort of."

"No, it's like the dance pavilion all over again."

Back when they were teens, Libby had led a campaign to save the Lake View Dance Pavilion. The place was ancient back when Libby was a kid. Libby led the charge in the 80s, when she was just fifteen, to turn it into a roller-skating rink on Friday nights. She'd been obsessed by it and had succeeded, at least for a time, in bringing tons of teens on wheels to the Lake View Dance Pavilion. They skated every Friday night. She'd crossed out dance and scrawled in skate on a bunch of fliers. It was one of her very first crusades.

"I was the biggest nerd in the world, even then."

"Nah, you had a vision, and all of us were happy to follow you!"

"That place is probably mothballed now after all that work. Nothing lasts."

"It's closed, but it is still there. And I'm still here, and you're here, and so is this house and the lake, so yes, some things do last if you fight for them."

Libby looked into Keith's eyes. She hadn't fought for Keith. Was that a little reminder? She didn't dare ask him to clarify.

"Right, sure. Still, how the heck am I going to fight this developer next week?"

"I have no doubt it'll come to you. And if you can't beat 'em, stall 'em until you can think of something."

"I have a lot of doubt. You know, I am here, after a colossal failure. I am not a success story, these days."

"I heard something about Henry?" Libby detected the old sneer that used to appear when Henry's name was mentioned. Keith sensed Henry was bad for her before she even did. And then she went and proved Keith right.

"Yeah, he liked to gamble and gambled with money from my non-profit."

"Trusting the wrong person, a lot of us have done that."

"You trusted me once. It turns out I was the wrong person to trust." All Libby could see were her missteps right now. One after another.

Keith looked at her, and for a split second, she saw the hurt she'd caused, decades ago, with a kiss from Henry.

"What are you doing today?"

Libby stepped back and fanned her hands over the pages of documents.

"I'm hoping a solution magically appears on these government papers."

"Get your bathing suit on."

"What?"

"Yeah, I'm taking you out on the water."

"It's still May. The idea of getting into that water is a non-starter."

"Get your suit on. We're going. You've got ten minutes."

Libby stood for a second, ready to argue about why this was a bad idea. Why she didn't have time. Why she was going to stay inside and fret.

Keith pointed to the hallway. It was clear from his comically firm expression that Libby was to march into that room and get her act together for a boat ride.

She tried not to smile at Keith and then did exactly as he had ordered her to do.

She put on her suit, pulled on a sweatshirt over it, and the cutoff jeans she'd taken to living in when she was here.

"How's this?"

"You're still a knockout if that's what you're fishing for."

"Stop. I mean, am I dressed okay for the weather conditions?"

"You'll be fine. Last I checked, you were made of tougher stuff than most super foxes."

"Foxes, oh boy, now we're really taking it way back."

They made their way to the boat.

Libby was in a time warp now. Floating off her old dock was a familiar sight. But it couldn't be! The shiny wood and gleaming metal made it look new. Except Libby knew this boat like the back of her hand.

"Oh my gosh! Is this the same boat?"

"Tis, my dad's old Chris-Craft, 1966 Vintage."

"How is this still old girl still so gorgeous?"

"She's like you. Age only helps."

"Please, I can't sneeze without needing a level five containment suit."

Keith laughed at Libby's candor. She wasn't going to put on airs with him. She didn't have to.

"She runs like a dream, too. There's this restoration place in Toledo, Ramsey Brothers. They're my go-to place for old parts and advice."

Keith put a hand out, and Libby put hers in his. She stepped aboard.

"Look at that steering wheel. I cannot believe it."

Libby had spent so much time on this boat, but it was a wreck back in the day. It was a cast-off Keith's dad let him use. Now it looked like it should be in a boat show! Libby found a spot next to the captain's seat. Actually, she wanted to ask to drive it, but she resisted. She should enjoy letting go once in a while. She needed to resist the urge to grab the steering wheel of every situation.

Keith started the engine, and they were off!

Manitou Lake was still fairly empty. Come July, boat traffic would be dense, but right now, there were maybe a dozen boats scattered throughout the fifteen-hundred-acre lake.

Libby had a pontoon boat in her garage. She had no idea if that worked. She made a note to check on it. Drifting slowly around the lake, catching the sun, having a cocktail was peak lake activity in her estimation. Though this trip in the Chris-Craft was an unexpected treat. Who knew that the vintage speed boat could double as a time machine?

They zipped around in circles a time or two. It was thrilling, a bit unhinged, and the opposite of who Libby was or had been since she left this place. There was a time when this was her summer. This was a thing she did all the time back then.

And then she saw them. The water skis.

And she wondered.

Keith pulled back on the throttle, and they slowed a bit. The engine was quiet enough now for Libby to ask.

"Did you plan on skiing today?"

"Actually, no. Early this morning, I was pulling the boys around. They challenge each other as to how early they can get in the water on 'em."

"Early in the morning?"

"No, how early in the season. We've got summer temperatures. A couple of years ago, they got on the lake in April, but the first week of May is pretty darn good."

"I'd say."

Libby made her way closer to the skis and then spied the wet suit.

"I mean, I know it won't fit right, but do you think?" She stopped short of voicing the complete question.

"Oh, THERE she is."

Keith's eyes were wide, and his handsome grin turned into a full-blown smile. Man, she needed to know what kind of toothpaste he used because those teeth were gorgeous.

Libby refocused on her flight of fancy. She whipped off her shorts and t-shirt. She stood there in her one-piece and concentrated on tugging on that wet suit. If you'd have asked her a year ago about getting mostly naked in front of a virtual stranger to go water skiing, she'd have said no. Hard no.

But if you'd have asked at sixteen, there wouldn't have been a second of hesitation. Libby pretended she was that version of herself. Keith's sons were tall and muscle-bound like he was, but she didn't care. She was tall, too. So what if the suit was a little big? Its purpose was to keep her from freezing to death, not for a photoshoot.

She dropped any pretense of gracefulness and shimmied into it. She turned with her back to Keith, and he zipped her up, no words between them. He knew how to aid and abet her adventurous side. They could read each other's minds once, and maybe today at least, they could again. It was as though they hadn't lived two lives since the last time they were out skiing together.

"Here."

Keith helped her pull on a life jacket. He tugged both sides and clipped it shut. It was intimate, Libby realized, and she looked up and into Keith's eyes. He, too, caught himself. She gave him a smile, and he finished clipping her vest around her.

"Have I lost my darn mind?"

"Nope, good day to try it. Water is glass, and there's no traffic."

"I used to be good at this," Libby said, more to bolster herself than to Keith.

"You used to do one ski, you used to barefoot! Good? You were *fantastic*, a water ski goddess!"

She laughed at the exaggeration.

"Is it like riding a bike?"

"We'll see. Get in there."

Libby jumped in that fast. She knew to ride this bold feeling, not to let it go, not to let the voice of reason return to her middle-aged brain.

The water was bracing, but the sun was warm, and the wetsuit did its job.

"Okay, here you go." Keith dropped the rope to her and then the skis.

She remembered how to do it, how to slide her feet in.

So far, it was like riding a bike.

Keith returned to the steering wheel and looked back at Libby. She had the rope in one hand, the tip of her skis pointed up in the water. She hoped they were positioned the right way. She gave Keith a thumbs up.

Here goes nothing.

Keith revved the engine. It seemed like the boat shot forward like a rocket.

Libby held tight to the rope, and for a fleeting second, she thought she had it, but she most definitely did not. Her legs weren't under her, and instead, they went in opposite directions. She let go of the tow line and realized that she had to have been a hilarious sight.

If her kids or her friends in Chicago could see her, they wouldn't believe this was buttoned-up Libby Malcolm.

She swam for the skis. Libby was grateful for her 5Ks and her Soul Cycle classes, as she didn't completely lose her breath while swimming.

"What do you want to do?"

"Try again. What else, K?"

"'Atta girl. Lean back a little more. I'll ease you up a bit, too. I'm used to full go with my boys."

Libby wanted to tell him to get bent and not to go easy on her. But that was sixteen-year-old bravado. Keith was right, she needed to better position herself, and he needed to remember she was a middle-aged woman who hadn't water skied in decades.

She got her act together and repositioned her skis. *Okay, old girl, you can do this!* A little self-pep talk didn't hurt.

She gave Keith the thumbs up again.

This time she was more prepared. She remembered, or her muscles did. She held tight to the tow and let her skis slide up, out of the water and then over it. For an awkward second, she faltered, but she leaned on her memory. She let her younger self take the wheel, and she was up.

Libby let out a little woot noise. She was up!

Her legs rattled, and the skis bounced over the water. But she held tight. She heard Keith yell, "Yahoo!" in answer to her expression of pure surprise and glee.

Water sprayed up to her face. She shook her head, and her hair whipped behind her.

The boat traveled a straight line through the middle of Lake Manitou, which was a nice long stretch. But it didn't last forever. It was time to turn, or the water would be too shallow for safety.

Libby remembered all of this, like no time had passed. Keith turned the boat left in a wide arc. The tow line swung out behind it. Libby had a moment of panic. She'd have to keep her balance and bump over the choppy foam of the wake.

She kept her head and stayed calm. She let her body handle the bounce but not be dislodged from her perch on the skis. She did it! She did it!

Now they were making a second pass down the easy centerline of the lake.

She was up for at least five minutes, three slow arcs. As she skied, she felt Keith push the throttle, and they went faster. Keith made the turn again at a higher speed. This time the wake bubbled under her skis with more energy. She felt her legs lose the idea of this endeavor.

Her grip was getting tough to maintain. She knew she couldn't hold it, so she let go of the line. She coasted over the water, gliding for a bit in a way that felt like flying.

There was no tow line, no boat, just her and the water, and the air. She splashed under, finally, and had a smile on her face. She gulped in a bit of lake water, but even that was okay. It was unsalted. She bobbed back up immediately, thanks to the life vest.

She looked up, and Keith was slowly bringing the boat around. She waved to let him know she was okay.

She lifted the skis, one at a time to Keith. He brought each onboard. He put out a hand and hoisted her up to the side of the boat. She had let go of the idea that she could be graceful getting on the boat. No one could, she realized, and all of a sudden, she didn't care. She'd done it. After decades and decades, she'd done it!

"Looked like you were having fun."

"Are you kidding? It was great! How have I not done this since the eighties?"

"Looks like it *was* like riding a bike."

"Maybe?"

The rush of her accomplishment had been keeping Libby warm. Despite the warm air, it was cold water. Her wet hair dripped it on her neck, and she started to shiver. She also didn't really care. Something had unlocked in her. That old confidence of youth, that idea that you could punch the sky, that thing that propelled her before life had weighed things down, rose up again in her chest.

"I cannot bbb-uh-lieve I could do it." Libby's teeth were now chattering.

"Get the suit off, get in this towel! You can't survive the water skiing only to get hypothermia."

Keith helped her peel out of the suit. Libby would have been mortified to think she'd let someone yank the thing off her legs, but she was done worrying about what looked proper. Or doing what was appropriate for a woman of a certain age. Keith was right. She was now freezing as she discarded the wetsuit.

"Here!" Keith wrapped her in a big beach towel.

The boat bobbed over the water, and Libby was tossed into Keith's arms.

He held on to her.

"You're warm. I need warm," she said, hoping she didn't sound stupid. At that moment, it was the dang truth. The confidence of youth also came with the awkwardness around old boyfriends, apparently. Keith and the towel did the job of bringing Libby's body temperature into a normal range.

"You did great," Keith said. And he looked into her eyes.

Libby realized that Keith might kiss her. What's more, she maybe wanted Keith to kiss her.

The moment passed. Libby straightened up and backed away slightly. There were enough life-changing events going on right now. She wasn't ready for one more. The morning had been magical, unique, and what she'd needed. Kissing someone? Kissing

Keith? That was magic she could save for another day, or not. If it was supposed to happen now or later, it would.

"Thank you. I don't know what came over me. I just had to try."

"My pleasure, and you did more than try. You did it, sliced it up out there. After your little blowout."

"Yeah, my legs were shaking. I am just grateful you had time to do this for me. I'll never forget it."

"You act like it's a one-time thing! Next time, one ski; after that barefooting. You were good at all three."

Libby laughed out loud. The girl she'd been was buried for so long, underneath the responsibilities of the woman she'd become —she'd need both versions of herself if she was going to pull off this next trick, saving Irish Hills.

And Keith had helped remind her that both were there, alive and well.

Libby was just getting started, darn it.

The day's adventure shook her out of her funk.

And it shook loose an idea.

Libby had a call to make, a big favor to ask, and a lot of work to do before the hearing.

The time on the water reminded her that she knew how to get her legs under her, and once she did, they were strong enough to navigate the wake.

Also, she made a note to buy some ibuprofen at the store.

Chapter Eighteen

Libby

Libby looked out at the empty stretch of lawn that stood between Nora House and the boathouse. There used to be a massive willow tree in the spot. That tree could have crushed the house during the tornado; instead, it fell on the boathouse.

She knew Aunt Emma had to have the tree removed in chunks.

Libby looked out to the boathouse. She realized that her aunt had done more than replace the roof. There was a better structure there now than what the tree took out. She hadn't had time to really explore it but knew there was even a little apartment up there. Aunt Emma called it the caretaker apartment. There was no caretaker to live in it now, but Libby wondered if it was rentable.

There were so many things to think about just with this house, but Libby had to focus. If she succeeded in staving off Stirling Development, maybe she could spend a week exploring her new home. But that would have to wait.

She was headed to town, and she was on a mission.

Aunt Emma owned a stretch of buildings downtown that Stirling had targeted. Stirling said they should be condemned. Aunt Emma had no means to fix the buildings but also refused to tear them down on her own. It really was a battle over the heart of downtown Irish Hills. If Libby could make that viable real estate...

This was where Libby knew she had the edge. She'd brought buildings back from the brink. She'd argued to save structures that others deemed a lost cause. And in so doing, she'd helped restore entire blocks, one address at a time.

Stirling Development planned to bulldoze the whole town, but their argument for that was based on specific properties that they'd surveyed and listed as obsolete, eye sores.

It was galling, really, that this out-of-town company could just decide what needed to go.

While Irish Hills suffered from a lack of clear leadership when it came to fixing this place up, it didn't mean some out-of-town money manager could come in and draw a big "x" through the map as he saw fit. It made her blood boil.

J.J.'s husband agreed to meet her downtown. In Libby's estimation, this was Emma's biggest problem, the fact that she owned this stretch and it looked terrible. If she could figure this out, maybe she would solve Emma's issue and have a fighting chance convincing the local government.

She'd pulled Dean off his normal job for the day and wanted him to know this wasn't for free. She planned to pay. She didn't know how, but if it came down to selling her jewelry, she'd do it.

"I will pay your normal rate; this is a big day or two of work. It's something I normally take weeks to do, but I need it done in hours."

"I'm here for the future work. If your plan pans out, it will more than pay for my next few days." Again, a person who had no reason to be sweet to her, or go out of their way, was doing just that.

"Thanks, Dean."

They got to work. Libby focused on the main street. If the five buildings listed as lost causes could be saved, she'd have neutralized at least one argument from the proposal.

There were five rentable spaces on one side of the street, seven more on the other, with a boulevard in the center. The gazebo used to hold local choir concerts and the like, and it too looked like a teardown.

Peck's Hardware was at the south end of Green Street and Barton's Food Village at the north end. Arrow Gas Station was next to the grocery store, and near Peck's was a small used car lot. That was the main drag. There was also a municipal building that would soon be the sight of Libby's last stand.

This was the hub. The key to slowing down Stone Stirling's plans was showing the mayor that Libby and the local business owners had a viable plan to save this little gem of a downtown.

A tarnished gem, to be sure. The entire block had been shuttered, some since the tornado and some over the last decade. The sidewalk had crumbled, and there was literally no reason for anyone to try to walk on it anyway.

She told Dean what she was after. Irish Hills would need viable, commercial retailers and restaurants right here, in buildings that Emma didn't have the cash to fix up. And from the looks of it, no one else could lease thanks to years of neglect.

"I need to know the foundation is okay. Electrical, roofing, siding, even plumbing is all on the table. I can fix those, but a foundation, well, that's gonna be tougher."

"Gotcha."

Dean climbed into crawl spaces and opened access panels. Libby and Dean donned respirator facemasks when he pulled open rotting drywall and exposed old insulation.

He poked the beams, used a ladder to inspect the roof, and crawled under every sink they could find.

Libby knew exactly what he needed to check. She'd done all of this before.

Finally, after a full day of poking around, the two of them met up with Jared and J.J. at the hardware store.

"You two look terrible," J.J. said, and her friend was right. Libby had cobwebs in her hair and dirt under her fingernails. She was sneezing dust that had collected in the buildings over decades.

"What's the verdict?" Jared asked.

J.J. handed them both a bottle of water as they sat in Jared's little break room at the back of the hardware store.

"The good news is the foundation of the northeast corner of the block is good. It is just as solid as it was back when it was built in 1919."

Libby felt a little surge of excitement. She didn't let it show, though. There was always a bad news component for this type of project.

"Wow, they look so terrible. It goes to show you that those masons of our great grandparents' generation were no joke. Amazing," Jared said.

"Yes, the floors were rotting, but pilings were strong, straight, and holding up those buildings, still, after all they've been through."

"Let's get to the but," Libby prompted.

"Yeah, the entire roof, from end to end, is a wreck. Total tear off. Then you've got no electrical. And the plumbing, I wish it was newer than the depression era. It isn't."

"No surprise there, no one's been keeping that up. It's been decades," J.J. said.

"You've basically got a shell, from end to end. That seasonal costume place comes in at Halloween, but really, it's a ghost town. And rightly so."

Dean slid his notes over to Libby. She scanned them.

"Okay, but, honestly, we could repair them. They wouldn't need to be leveled?"

"No, I mean new everything, but that block could be saved, it just costs more than anyone here has, or any business is willing to invest."

"I know you can't give me exact numbers but are we under a million?"

Dean looked at her like she was speaking a different language all of a sudden. It crushed Libby. She'd lowballed what it would take, by a mile, from the way Dean was looking at her when she asked to ballpark the numbers.

"A million, you say?"

"Ugh, double that?" Libby had a number in mind, a way to afford the revitalization, but if it was several million, well, her grand idea was a non-starter.

"J.J., I think we need to move to Chicago," Dean said.

"What?" J.J. said.

"If that's what they're paying contractors in the Windy City, we'd be millionaires in a summer!"

Libby was now completely confused.

"Wait, what are you saying?" Libby asked Dean.

"I'm saying it's not double a million. It's half, and then half again." Libby could hardly believe her ears.

"Wait, so, you're talking 250-thousand to fix that block, to make those repairs?"

"Yes, still a king's ransom, but a couple million? Wow, you're really used to getting charged through the nose, like I said. I'm in the wrong part of the country. Two million, oh boy."

Libby's heart soared; this was great news. With the numbers Dean had just quoted, she could do it. She knew she could. She couldn't do it in a day, and there were hoops to jump through, but her mind raced. She knew she could put together a grant proposal that would knock the socks off the Small Business Downtown Revitalization Authority. They were the agency that helped small towns, just like Irish Hills.

She'd gotten three times that amount before, for one building alone.

Phase one of Stone Stirling's argument was about to be cut off at the knees!

Libby stood up and wrapped her arms around Dean's burly frame. She squeezed.

"This is awesome news, awesome!"

"Seriously? That's the highest quote I've ever been near, and she's thrilled," Dean said with a laugh.

"Okay, I better go write this up!"

Libby couldn't wait to get to her laptop. She still had two more big pillars to knockdown. But thanks to Dean, one obstacle had just been managed. It wasn't a done deal but darn it, Libby was on the low end of the grant ask with this. She was more hopeful than she'd been in several days.

It felt good to know she really could help.

She had less than four days to go before the meeting and a million things to do, but the good news was the fuel she needed to get to the finish line. With Dean's assessment, Libby crafted a grant request.

She knew the ins and outs of getting grant money, and that was her play for downtown.

Getting grant money for development in a big city was different than a small town, but Libby was a pro. She spent the next twenty-four hours writing, compiling, and making a few phone calls.

She also called in every favor she was owed.

After twenty years of community development work, of homes saved, community centers revitalized, and early childhood programs funded, Libby had more than a few names on her list. She may be a pariah when it came to getting a job, but she had a contacts file full of people who'd benefited from her work.

If nothing else, she'd learned that from Aunt Emma. Leverage everything you can when you're up against the wall.

* * *

Libby's other project was the gas station situation. Stirling Development argued that Arrow's little place was behind the times.

She'd made her calls on that right away, after her water-skiing epiphany. She knew what to do to help Arrow's gas station. That one was mercifully easy to pull off. And she had set the wheels in motion for a grant for renovating Aunt Emma's stretch of downtown buildings, thanks to Dean's appraisal it was doable.

Now she needed to figure out one more thing.

And it might be the hardest, with the clock ticking down to the day of the meeting.

How would they bring people to Irish Hills? The lakes weren't a problem. People showed up in droves for those, but why come to Irish Hills for anything else when you could go to bigger towns or big boxes? How could she entice the cottage renters, the summer people, to come here instead of somewhere else? How do you ensure that if businesses are revitalized, customers show up?

She'd spent one day surveying property and the next on the phone or on her laptop. There was still so much to do.

Finally, Libby got in her Jeep after twenty-four hours of hunching over her laptop. Sometimes a change of scenery helped bring her new ideas. Water-skiing had worked. Maybe a quick drive would, too.

She didn't have a plan or a destination. What she had was motivation to find something, anything, to help stave off the development plans. Progress wasn't bad, it was good, but there were plenty of places you could go to if you wanted an all-inclusive resort or cookie-cutter condos. There weren't many places like this, places with history, cottages that you could afford even if you weren't a millionaire, and mom and pop B&Bs dotting every lake.

Libby drove the two-lane roads that wrapped lazily around the low hills, she turned down gravel drives, she stopped at the public beach at Little Stoney Lake.

She drove past Vineyard Lake. The water was Caribbean blue!

Even in the few short weeks she'd been here, the trees had turned from buds to full blossoms. Keith was right. Mother Nature was doing her best to make summer happen early this year.

She eventually found the old Lake View Dance Pavilion.

The sign was dilapidated, hanging off to one side by a rusty chain. Weeds had grown over a path to the entrance.

Irish Hills Country Club might be home to fancy events for people who paid big bucks to be members. But all you needed to attend a dance at Lake View was two dollars.

Lake View Dance Pavilion was only a quarter of a mile away from downtown Irish Hills. It wasn't even mentioned in the Stirling Proposal.

Libby could understand why. If you didn't know it was here, you'd drive right by.

Keith had reminded her of her big campaign to turn this into a groovy skating rink back in her day. Libby had saved this place once. And maybe it would have survived longer if the tornado hadn't hit, but here it was, now a skeleton.

There was a huge outdoor dance floor for when the weather cooperated. But the real draw was the giant a-frame structure. Libby remembered it had a small kitchen, a bar, an upper balcony, and a big stage. Rain, shine, or hail, you could go inside and dance your brains out. You didn't need to belong to anything. All you needed were your dancing shoes or skates!

Libby walked further into the property and up onto the cement platform. Her mind floated backward.

She could hear the boom box blaring for their skate parties.

1988, Lake View Dance Pavilion

The mixtape Goldie had made was so perfect! It was the eighties, but they spent a fair amount of time disco roller skating to seventies tunes. They lifted their arms to form YMCA and struggled to catch themselves when they lost balance.

And then Goldie snuck in 'Hungry Eyes' by Eric Carman, and it was a whole 'nother thing. Keith grabbed Libby by the hand, and they were couple skating!

For a second, Libby remembered thinking about her Sandbar Sisters as she and Keith rounded the floor on their skates. They were going to grill her about this. Hope was mercifully also couple skating, Goldie, too. That was good, she thought. Because J.J. and Viv would ask a million embarrassing questions. Maybe they'd spread it around to Hope and Goldie.

Keith was asking her something.

They laughed about something else.

And for the entire song, Keith and Libby held hands. They were in sync. And Libby decided that if the opportunity ever presented itself, Keith would be 'the one.'

Libby scandalized herself with the thought!

Keith was a good partner. He guided them around the rink, slid by slower couples, and kept her steady over that one little notch in the concrete they kept passing.

The slow song was over. It shifted to George Michael's 'Monkey.' Goldie's favorite that summer.

Libby was reluctant to stop holding hands with Keith. He seemed to think the same thing. He leaned in and kissed her, not during the dopey slow song but during George Michael. Goldie was going to be so confused.

Afterward, as expected, the girls gathered at Nora House. They talked into the morning about the couple skate, the cute boys that were there, the time J.J. nearly chipped a tooth when she "biffed it."

Aunt Emma supplied the girls with a snack at whatever god-awful hour it was.

"Ah, the Pavilion, we used to have USO dances there during

the war," Aunt Emma said as she passed out the Rice Krispie Treats, she'd made. The girls ignored it. The USO?

They stayed up all night, recounting every single second. Each song, each handhold, and all the tiny details of their night on wheels.

* * *

Libby hadn't thought about these moments in so long. This was the place a lot had changed for her.

She walked around the pavilion, stepped over weeds, tugged on the rusty lock that kept the door to the beat up old building shut. What purpose could the lock possibly serve at this point?

There was a for sale sign on the side of the structure. Libby knew the auction house listed on the sign specialized in last chance properties. That was certainly the case here, an old dance pavilion, a slab of concrete, next to a town that no one was visiting. It didn't exactly scream that it was a desirable real estate commodity.

Then her aunt's words, mentioned off-hand, to a gaggle of giggling teen girls.

"Ah, the Pavilion, we used to have USO dances there during the war."

Libby took a picture of the real estate auction sign. She needed that phone number.

Libby's mind was fevered, again, with an idea. One that could be another way to prop up Irish Hills and stave off Stone Stirling's plan to pave everything over.

This was just as pie in the sky as the rest of Libby's ideas, but it could be the missing piece she needed.

Chapter Nineteen

Emma

Libby was back and had a million questions, along with a musty old box.

She was calmer. That was something. And Emma noticed that Libby was less worried about herself and more worried about the task at hand. That was a good sign!

It had just taken a little push.

"So good to see you, dear. I didn't think you'd have time for a visit, what with the meeting coming up."

"This is about that," Libby said.

"Oh, good then. I hope all is progressing nicely."

"Aunt Emma, I am going to have to throw a Hail Mary pass at that meeting. Make no mistake about it, but I'll give it my best."

"Your arms look strong."

"Here's what I need. I need you to remember everything you can about the Lake View Dance Pavilion."

"Oh, dear, your little roller rink pet project."

"Yes, that was the eighties, and the place was struggling even back then. But Owen Green owned it, then, and he let us do our roller-skating revival thing."

"Before Owen, Charlie O'Riley built it, and he added the balcony. Goodness, he really brought in the bands! And then, of course, the tornado, yes, so terrible. It was such a good idea you had. Too bad your skating thing was so short-lived."

Libby waved off the mention of the skating rink. "Okay, so, I remember you mentioning the USO dances and musical acts back in the fifties?"

"Oh, long before then. That place is older than I am, by a good bit! Father donated some of the concrete. I remember him saying that."

"Okay, yes, I did some research. It was built in 1914, so we're looking at a structure that has been there over one hundred years."

"It isn't polite to mention how old I am in relation to that, dear."

"Aunt Emma, I've got an idea, but I need some proof, backstory, and a few other things to make this fly."

"But it's about saving Irish Hills?"

"It is."

"I used to square dance there, and mother and father went on a few dates there. Also, I heard the McFarland Twins and The Victors play there."

"Which are, what, bands?"

"Yes, but boy, mother and I had a big quarrel when I snuck out to the pavilion to see Tommy Dorsey."

"Okay, now, I've heard of him. He was big in the Big Band era?"

"He was very famous."

Libby opened the box that she'd brought. It was filled with old photographs that Emma hadn't thought of in years.

"How ever did you find these? I'd forgotten about all these."

"I was up in the attic, exploring, and well, this is a drop in the bucket."

"We're an old family. I just never knew what to do with all this."

"Okay, so, is this you?"

Libby handed her a photo. Emma was in her favorite navy-blue dress, with the red belt. Her bag and shoes matched. Of course, Emma's mother did not like those red shoes. She was standing outside the dance pavilion. Her date, whose name she could not remember for the life of her, had taken the photo.

"It sure is, we were going to see Guy Lombardo. That was during the war. I remember that."

Libby nodded. She took a file folder and produced a pen from her bag. "We're going to go through this box. It is pretty much all pertaining to things that happened in the war years. I need you to help me label this."

"Oh, I am not one for living in the past. We're in a very real crisis right now. There isn't time to walk down memory lane—or Lindy Hop down it." Emma chuckled at her own little joke.

"Aunt Emma, trust me on this. The fact that the dance pavilion had all these history-making acts back in the 1930s and 1940s could very much help us today."

"Okay, well, past my time, they also had...what's the fellow's name? Roy Orbison! And that Little Miss Dynamite, Brenda Lee."

Libby's mouth dropped open like she was trying to catch flies.

"Wow, okay, wow. Let's get into it."

After two hours of work, Emma got tired, but they'd gotten through the box. Libby took every photo, ticket stub, and playbill and carefully placed it in a file with an appropriate label.

"I think that's a good start. There is a lot more up in that attic."

"Mostly just faded memories, I thought."

"Or, actual history," Libby said. It appeared she was talking more to herself than to Emma.

"Whatever you say, dear."

"What I have to figure out now is who owns Lake View Dance

Pavilion. There's a for-sale sign on it that's rotting away. It must have been up for sale forever."

"That's easy enough. You do."

"What?"

"Yes, a few years ago, I bought it from Ned Barton. He'd bought it from Owen Green. Ned had plans to expand, maybe even move the grocery store out there. It is quite large. But Ned got behind, like everyone else. So, instead of going into foreclosure, I took it off his hands. Didn't you look at all the documents Patrick provided? I'm sure the pavilion deed is in there somewhere."

"And it's been sitting there, sign in the dirt, rotting?" Libby looked at once incensed at the news and excited.

"Well, I've bailed just about everyone out around her at one point or another. That's why I need your help. There's a hole in the bucket, Dear Liza, Dear Liza."

"Okay, okay, what else do you own, Aunt Emma?"

"Dear, while I own that stuff downtown and a few other things, *you* own the pavilion. I threw it in. It should be in the list Patrick gave you."

"Oh my, I really should have looked at the fine print."

To be fair to her niece, Emma had hornswoggled her. Emma had wanted Libby to be too busy to really look at what she was saying yes to. It was part of the plan, and it really had worked spectacularly.

"Yes, yes, you should have, uh—oh, the taxes will be next year. I took care of this year, but, as you know, my cash flow has dried up."

"I need to get some income, somehow to pay this. Yep, I got it, Aunt Emma."

"But the history thing, that's good, right?"

Emma watched her niece give her a now-familiar look of exasperation.

"Yes, yes, it is. I hope. I think."

Emma stared at Libby. "I know you're frustrated with me, I can see that, but you aren't so down in the mouth. You've bucked up. This has been the perfect thing for you."

Libby narrowed her eyes at Emma, who hoped her niece wouldn't bring up the unpleasantness with that man in the tornado.

"I suppose, yes, I'm feeling better. Despite your blackmail and backing me into a corner."

Darn, oh well, Emma wasn't a hothouse flower. She wasn't going to wither with a word.

"Oh, the best thing about being backed into a corner is you only have one way out."

"Yeah," Libby conceded.

"So, start punching, my dear. Start punching."

Chapter Twenty

Libby

Dean and Jared had proved to be lifesavers.

They helped cart in and set up Libby's visual aids. And they fixed the darn easel thing when it kept sliding down. Libby had facts, along with her visual aids, and she had letters of intent.

Libby had prepared. She had rehearsed.

The Mayor of Irish Hills was a man named Chet Eastland. The three city council members were Tammy Krouse, Earl Shot, and Don Keller. They'd all had a history in Irish Hills. Libby didn't know them personally, but she hoped that was a sign they felt connected to the past.

They were going to get the full force of Libby's efforts over the last week.

"Your posters look very great. You look like a Viking Warrior Princess. They'll be on board before you even finish your presentation. I promise."

J.J. was playing the role of hype man.

"I look that terrified?"

"I just said—"

"You don't lavish compliments on a person who looks like they have no fear."

"Yeah, your shaking, pacing, and mumbling sort of gave that away."

"I want to be perfect."

"Aha! That's the old Libby. You are way too hard on yourself. This town doesn't need perfect. It needs a few queens like you."

"And you, crooked crowns and all?"

"Exactly."

"I'm going to find a seat right behind you. This place is starting to fill up. Man, I should have set up a popcorn stand or something."

"K."

Libby looked behind her and saw the truth of that. Dean and Jared were there, but she spied several more familiar faces filling the rows. And then her eyes found Keith, who was flanked by two handsome young men. His sons? They looked like him and also didn't.

They had a good portion of their mother in them. Libby was reminded again how bruised they all must be, after losing their mom. She nodded her head in gratitude.

She was relieved to see there weren't any TV stations here. They were in a no man's land of news coverage, between Toledo and Detroit. Her recent experiences with the press weren't pleasant so no news was good news in her estimation.

Her Aunt Emma made a grand entrance with Patrick.

She had a seat up front, next to Libby.

"This is going to be so fun," enthused Emma.

"No, not at all, these things are dry and plodding, the opposite of fun."

Aunt Emma waved a hand in dismissal of Libby's characterization of the pending presentation.

And in walked Clyde Brubaker, still wearing his logoed golf shirt.

He looks more puffed up than before, more confident than he should, Libby thought.

"Oooh, who's that handsome one with Clyde?"

Libby locked eyes with the developer. She'd met him on the conference call and seen pictures of him posing at Stirling Resorts, but there was no mistaking who strode in behind Clyde.

He was tall, wore a gray business suit that was likely more expensive than the entire repair bill of downtown Irish Hills, and had a jawline that could cut glass. He was flanked by what Libby assumed was an attorney, also suited up for battle.

"Crap," Libby said under her breath. If Clyde Brubaker was filled with false confidence, it was easy to see the source.

Stone Stirling was brimming with world-beater energy. He was used to getting exactly what he wanted. And right now, he wanted to take this town and make it a gateway to a resort that he would build, control, and make big money from. Libby and the people who lived here were little bumps in the road.

"Good thing you put on the dog. That man is handsome!" Aunt Emma whispered into her ear.

"Shh!" Her aunt's whisper wasn't really a whisper.

Still, Libby was also relieved that she'd selected the one remaining power suit she'd held onto in the event she needed to attend a funeral or job interview. This was feeling a lot like a combination of both.

Mayor Eastland and the three city council members arrived, sat down, and arranged various papers in front of them. A clerk looked to the mayor, who nodded.

The clerk read from the prepared agenda.

"This is a hearing to decide on a timeline for the eminent domain proposal from Stirling Development Company. The proposal calls for phase one to begin in the next thirty days, whereby Stirling Development will assess values for properties in the proposed zone. Attorney Grant Mills is here on behalf of Stirling to outline the proposal in front of this body."

Attorney Grant Mills? Ah, the other well-suited man sitting with Clyde and Stone.

Libby knew what was in the proposal. She could recite it herself after poring over it for hours. The attorney for Stirling stood up, buttoned his expensive suit coat, went to the lectern in front of the assembled elected officials, and began speaking.

"You've all received our proposal and have expressed support, which we appreciate. We look forward to working with everyone here. Our plan is to offer market value for all the outstanding structures and businesses listed, and this process will be expedited quickly so everyone involved will have a smooth transition out of the area before our infrastructure work begins."

The council members and mayor flipped through the glossy materials as Grant Mills continued.

"This would facilitate the area being ready by the end of the summer so that our foundation work can begin before the colder months set in this fall and winter."

"Thank you, and now we'll give the floor to Libby Quinn Malcolm—uh, Mrs. Malcolm, this doesn't state your title, if you could?"

Libby stood up. Her suit wasn't worth the same coin as Stirling's or Mills', but she knew it fit her well. With her hair tightly wound on her head and her pearl stud earrings, at the very least, she looked like it wasn't her first rodeo.

She hoped her plans and presentation backed up her stagecraft.

"Yes, I'm here as a Community Development Coordinator. I also own or represent the owners of several of the properties listed in this proposal." She dropped the proposal on the lectern as those it was hot garbage.

Libby decided not to correct the clerk on whether she was Mrs. Malcolm. She was here to win them over, not explain how she hated being called Mrs. Malcolm, with a white-hot intensity of a thousand suns.

"I, too, have read the proposal. There are three points that Stirling Development makes to argue that Irish Hills is no longer a viable community. I'd like to address those points and then, of course, answer any questions."

They all nodded, and Libby got to work.

"The first point outlines a concern that there is no modern fueling center here or within a reasonable distance from Irish Hills. The argument for construction is economic and environmental. While it is true Arrow Gas Station is the only fueling center, other than Keith Brady's Marina, this issue is about to be off the table."

"How so?" asked Mayor Eastland.

Libby walked to the first rendering she had prepared. This was the first thing she'd put in place, the first favor she'd called in.

"We Go Fuel Stop recently entered into an agreement with Arrow Orwig to invest in his operation here. We Go Fuel is a well-known chain of state-of-the-art, independent fuel centers in the state of Illinois. Reginald Bellamy, the CEO, is interested in expanding and will do so first, here, in Irish Hills. The service center will continue to operate downtown but will also expand to offer charging stations and E85, as it does in its other locations."

"What?" Libby believed that was Grant Mills, interrupting, not at all politely or quietly. She ignored it.

"We've provided copies of the letter of intent." J.J. was ready to go, and she handed the clerk half a dozen copies of the initial agreement between Arrow Orwig and Reginald Bellamy's company.

This was the payoff Reggie had promised. Her old friend had understood how hard it was for Libby to step down from her own non-profit in Chicago. He'd recognized that she'd done it for the greater good. Fighting to stay CEO would have taken away from all she was trying to do for the community. He was a good man, and he'd respected her actions in the worst moments of her life.

When Libby called, Reginald Bellamy had answered and

agreed that Irish Hills was a perfect location to begin his plans to branch out of Illinois.

She let that information sit for a second, walked over to the first visual aid she'd prepared, and took the covering off to reveal an updated gas station.

The council members, mayor, and community members craned their necks to see, but Libby pushed on.

"The next area I'd like to address is the northeast corner of the main street. Those buildings are listed as beyond repair in Stirling's proposal. A trained and licensed building inspector spent several days assessing the condition. Based on those assessments, it is clear from the documents J.J. Tucker is handing out now that the structures are simply not in as dire condition as their reports state. The foundations are intact, the issue is roofing, electrical, and plumbing, no doubt, but the structures themselves are prime downtown commercial real estate and are ripe for redevelopment and rehabilitation, not demolition. In fact, as the second page indicates, I've begun the process of securing grants to fund that project. Now those do take a few months to process, but the possibility is rather strong that Irish Hills will be eligible for upwards of five hundred thousand dollars in grant funding to handle all those repairs listed."

She paused for a second to let that sink in.

"My aunt, Emma Libby," Libby went on, "owns the property and is excited to begin those renovations. Here are some renderings to give you an idea of the direction of those plans."

Libby walked over to her second visual aid. She pulled the small sheet off the easel to reveal a rendering of the rehabilitated stretch of buildings. Stirling had proposed they all be bulldozed.

The potential was obvious. There could be a restaurant, a bakery, even a little shop or two. They could. The plan was possible. Viable even. That's all Libby was trying to show. They could, and it wouldn't cost millions.

"Stirling has painted downtown as a lost cause, as an obvious blight on the area, but it clearly isn't. In fact, the costs of renovation are reasonable. Not only that, but they are also perfectly aligned with a national push to save small-town commercial districts. Tearing down viable buildings to make way for a highway exit and rest area is not."

Libby had saved her best play for last.

She knew there would be questions and arguments from Stirling's mouthpiece, and she was ready.

"I have a few more items, but Mr. Mills seems to want to jump in here," Libby said. She stayed calm, unconcerned. She'd let the lawyer seem hysterical as she calmly answered.

"This is all well and good, but there is no guarantee that this downtown development grant will come through. Mrs. Malcolm is delivering a fanciful idea—from out of town, I might add—that has no impact on this project and the plans here."

"It's Ms. Quinn, Libby Quinn, to be specific. My family has deep ties to the area. In fact, it's that part that I do want to discuss next."

"Before I let you do that," Mr. Mills rushed on, "let's also remember that every single business owner is struggling in this place. They'd get market value and be able to cash out."

"Yes, market value. Your company has a vested interest in devaluing everything in this town. That way, you can buy everyone out, at a bargain, and then build up your resort so that the only one who actually profits here is Stirling Development."

"Your own pitch just let us know how inexpensive those buildings on the main street actually are."

"I said the repairs are not astronomical, not that the buildings weren't valuable. The fact is you've inflated the costs of repairs, so you can deflate the cost to buy them."

"That's ridiculous. You're selling these people a bill of goods, that you're going to redevelop a restaurant and a gas station, and poof, they'll have a business."

"Actually, thank you for bringing that up. The final thing I want to let you all know about is the Lake View Dance Pavilion."

J.J. looked for her cue, but Libby gestured a slight 'no, just wait.'

"Through my Aunt Emma Ford Libby, who many of you know, I am now the owner of the Lake View Dance Pavilion. It is, of course, in disrepair. And suffering from the blight that Stirling has ascribed to other areas of town."

"Good Lord, how long is she going to blather on?" Grant Mills interrupted, speaking directly to the people in the audience. "Let's get this vote so we can get your checks processed."

Libby knew the townspeople weren't the sort to be swayed by the big city or the promise of a quick buck. They'd been here all along. They knew the town. They knew this was a place of unique beauty.

Libby was not concerned that Grant Mills or Stirling would win anymore, at least not with the people sitting in the chairs. They were on her side. She still had to finish her presentation and hoped that would be enough for the politicians.

"Let the lady finish!" came a cry from somewhere in the audience.

Politicians were the same no matter what the size town.

The mayor sensed, as Libby did, that the room was hers, at least for now. He piped up for the first time. "I agree. Please, Ms. Quinn, continue. You still have the floor."

"Thank you, as I was saying, I am now the owner of the Lake View Dance Pavilion, thanks to my aunt, who, at a very young ninety, would like to step back from some of her many civic and community activities. Many of you here, of course, are aware of all she's done for Irish Hills. As the new owner of the Lake View Dance Pavilion, I'm announcing that it is my aim to restore it to its former glory."

"Former glory? It's a heap." This time it was Clyde Brubaker who interjected. He was from the area. He did know that the pavilion was a shell of a place and a venue long past its prime.

"Shut it, Clyde, or I'll get your grandmother," Aunt Emma said. "She will box your ears with one hand without missing a beat on her bingo card." It was no idle threat, Rose Brubaker and Emma were thick as thieves these days at Silver Estates.

Everyone nodded at that assertion as if it was a fact you could take to the bank.

"So, about the pavilion," Libby continued coolly, "Mr. Hill's point is well made. We can renovate the downtown and, of course, bring in the modern fueling station, but that doesn't bring in foot traffic for our local businesses. As the pavilion owner, I'm working on a several-pronged solution to that. First, the site is, without question, of historical significance. And as such, it needs to be protected, forever, as a historical landmark. The second prong will be to bring in the biggest musical acts in the country."

"What? Right, they're gonna come to Irish Hills?"

"Yes, they are. If it was good enough for Roy Orbison, I'm pretty sure it will be good enough for Chris Stapleton. Faster Horses, just ten miles up the road, has shown that tens of thousands of country music fans are willing to flock to the region. This is a great place for music fans. Between that and a few other ideas, within a season or two, this place will be THE place for summer fun."

"Which is our plan, why we're here," Grant claimed.

"It seems as if you're here to push these fine people out, and the cottages, and the local inns. After that payday, where will they be? Because you'll be here raking it in. You absolutely know that we have a beautiful and untapped resource in Irish Hills. You're doing this because it's valuable, not because it's a lost cause. I'm offering a pathway for the local businesses to benefit. For the local people to thrive."

Libby looked to J.J. and gave her the 'yes' nod, and with that, the last rendering was revealed. It showed an overview of the town, with the revitalized downtown Irish Hills, and a fixed-up pavilion.

It looked a lot like the Irish Hills she remembered, not the one leveled by a once-in-a-century tornado.

There was a whistle in the crowd.

"If there are any questions, I'm happy to answer," Libby said.

"I, for one," said Grant Mills, "would like to point out that a historical designation doesn't just happen because you've announced it. You can't—what's the word?— manifest it."

"Is that the question, is manifest the word? It is a word. I can confirm." Libby got a good laugh out of that.

"I am saying your ridiculous ideas are just that, fantasies from someone who has no idea if or how to make them happen."

"Well, to the comment about the historical designation, that process is straightforward, especially since I own the property. The level of musical talent that performed here is a who's who of the history of big band, country, rockabilly, and early rock and roll. The structure is over one hundred years old and quite important. So, I've no doubt that the designation will be awarded. This document outlines the requirements for the designation and protections associated with it, including protections from bulldozers and steam rollers."

"Ha!" This time the interruption was from J.J. Libby tried not to smile in response.

"It's nearly criminal the level of fraud you're perpetrating upon these innocent townspeople," Grant Mills sneered. "I didn't want to bring this up, but this woman was drummed out of her last non-profit for embezzling."

There was a ruffle in the room. Here it was, the full-on assault of her character that she knew would come.

"Is this true?" the mayor interjected.

"If I may, I voluntarily stepped down from my non-profit in the wake of a scandal. My husband at the time did embezzle. I was unaware of his activities. But I did not want to sully the community development efforts due to my association with him. There are documents to show all of this. There's a search engine called

Google that Mr. Mills might not be aware of that will show all that. Remember, two 'l's in Malcolm."

That got a little laugh. Libby had defanged the accusation by acting like it was nothing.

"How do we know that won't happen here? It seems a huge breach of judgment," asked Mayor Eastland.

"I divorced his ass and changed the locks." This came out of Libby's mouth with no thought or plan, and she heard it like someone else was speaking. It didn't go with her buttoned-up professional mode at all.

But it worked.

The collected citizenry of Irish Hills clapped and cheered. Libby turned around to look. Keith and his sons were clapping, Dean was belly laughing, and even sour-faced Ned Barton had a smile on his face.

"Looks like you've developed quite the community here this week," Aunt Emma remarked. She was smiling. It was smug, like she knew along that this was the right place for Libby.

"The woman is not to be trusted," Mills blurted.

"This is my area of expertise. I do not want to brag or toot my own horn, but I am the recipient of several national honors in relation to my work in this specific area."

That's when J.J. held up a poster Libby had never seen and absolutely did not authorize.

"It's not bragging if you can do it," said J.J.

The picture clearly showed Libby, Oprah Winfrey, Bono, and George W. Bush at a community service awards presentation. Libby's Southtown Now project had been honored at a fancy awards dinner. It was one of the highest honors of her professional career.

"Where did you get that?" Libby hissed at J.J.

"Google, it's a popular search engine."

Libby laughed and shook her head.

"If you think you—"

Grant Mills was clearly about to continue hurling insults, but Stirling Stone put a hand on the arm of his mouthpiece. He gave him a look that clearly conveyed the directive: *Shut up!*

Grant Mills shut up, but he didn't want to. He was angry that Libby and J.J. had bested him.

Mayor Eastland spoke up. "I think we have enough to vote. As Donna said, we're voting on allowing Stirling Development to fast track their plans for eminent domain, so that's a yes vote. Or voting to hold off, six months, a no vote. This does not torpedo the project as we understand it. It just slows it down."

Libby returned to a seat between her aunt and J.J. She felt a few pats on the back as she settled in. Her adrenaline was pumping. She'd done all she could with a week to prepare. She'd fought the good fight in front of a huge company with a billion dollars and access to dozens of lawyers.

"All in favor of allowing Stirling Development to move forward with the valuation stage of their proposal for repurposing Irish Hills, Councilwoman Krouse," the council clerk called for the votes.

"Yes."

Libby swallowed hard. Apparently, she hadn't won the room.

"Councilman Keller?"

"Yes."

Libby sank in her chair. This was a disaster. She felt like an idiot. Where was Bono when you needed him?

"Councilman Shot?"

"No."

"The vote is two to one in favor of allowing the current eminent domain to stay in place. The mayors' vote would tie it, but as we know, it also breaks the tie," said the clerk.

"Mayor Eastland?"

This was it. All the frenzy of work Libby had done, her restored confidence, her grand plans, it was all about to go down the drain.

"Oh, Lord, he's gonna talk," Aunt Emma said.

And she was right.

The mayor leaned into his microphone and talked. And talked. He mentioned civic pride, history, the future, his love of the Irish Hills, his love of the good corporate citizens like Stirling Development. He continued on to mention his love of country music and American-made products. There appeared to be no end in sight for his oration.

"What we're hearing is your love of your own voice. I'm 90-years-old. I don't have until next month to listen. What's your vote?"

Leave it to Aunt Emma to cut to the chase!

Mayor Eastland choked a bit and had the decency to look embarrassed by Aunt Emma's assessment of what he actually loved.

"I am voting against the development, and as the mayor, my tie-breaker vote also means this project will be delayed for six months."

The mayor banged a gavel. There was a cheer from behind her. She'd done it. They'd done it! They'd beat back the developer!

Libby looked over at Stone Stirling in the midst of the celebrating. He returned her gaze.

There was a small smile in the corner of his mouth. While Grant Mills and Clyde Brubaker were furious, Stirling Stone looked almost pleased.

Billionaires are so weird.

Libby worried about what that smile meant for a second, but she was soon overcome with hugs and handshakes.

They had done it, at least for now.

They'd saved Irish Hills from the wrecking ball and even found a way forward if Libby could come through on the promises she'd just made. But she'd bought time.

Hopefully, it was enough.

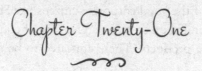

Chapter Twenty-One

Emma

The three women sat on the porch, no old boyfriends, no lawyers, no handsome developers. Just two of the famous Sandbar Sisters of Lake Manitou and one wily old lady. Emma didn't mind being the wily old lady.

She rather liked it.

The sun was setting. It was a view Emma had seen a million times, but it was never the same view twice. There was always a different hue to the sky, one night pink, another orange, the next gray. There were endless colors in the sky and in the lake's waters.

Thanks to Libby, there would be decades to come where new families could see this, appreciate it from the little cottages, from porches not too different from this one.

"Aunt Emma, you know what we're here for?" Libby asked.

"Lemonade? You're getting good at making it, dear."

"No, not lemonade."

"Oh, okay, you're wanting to know what I have on you and your feral pack of eighties teenage girls."

The two younger women wanted to laugh, Emma could see, but they were worried. Emma knew she'd brought out the big guns when she threatened to float the story of the man they left out in the tornado.

Actually, now, looking at the two of them, she felt a pang of guilt. These were sweet women, good girls—spirited then and now, sure, but they weren't murderers. Though, they didn't know they weren't.

That was Emma's edge. If they knew, would they be less bold or more? Emma wondered for a moment if doing what they did made them or broke them.

"How did you know about Bruce?" J.J. asked her.

"You know I am friends with everyone in town. We heard the stories about how your mother got the shiner and how he tanned your brother's hide."

"Yeah, he was a real piece of work, but still," J.J. said.

"Not sorry to see him swept up in the maelstrom of the tornado, were ya?"

"Aunt Emma, we were afraid," Libby said. "We made a split-second decision—*I* made a split-second decision—not to let him in."

"We all did, Libby. Stop acting like it was just you," J.J. said. "You were always putting way too much on your shoulders, still are."

Emma admired the friendship these two women had rediscovered. She sent up a little prayer of gratitude for the friends she still had and the ones she'd made at Silver Estates. And also, for the ones whom she'd lost. She imagined them all here, watching the sunsets with a cold drink.

"Look, I did what you asked. We have bought some time for Irish Hills here. But I need you to level with us. What do you have, what do you know, about Bruce?" Libby needed the truth. Emma knew that.

"You needed a push in the right direction. I gave you that, is all."

"Aunt Emma, you as much as said you were going to tell authorities we murdered that guy."

"I did? You know, I am old. Sometimes things get fuzzy."

The two younger women looked at each other, they didn't buy it, but that was okay. Emma was sticking to it. That was the best part of being over ninety. It could be true. She might have forgotten!

"Aunt Emma, spill it."

"The truth is, I was there. I saw you young ladies close the door."

"You were where?"

"I was trying to get to the house as that beast came our way. I was going to scream at you all to get in the cellar. Instead, I found Bruce. That was his name, right? I found him locked out."

"You found him?"

"That I did. I watched that twister miss the house. I watched the tree I'd swung on as a little girl lift up by the roots and fly across the sky. I had driven up in my car, lucky it didn't get sucked up. I was sitting there, frozen, really. No way to fight a twister in your front yard. At that point, there was nothing to be done. A tornado is capricious, it hits and skips, and if it hits, you're dead. If it skips, sometimes not even a scratch."

"But you saw," Libby prompted.

Emma watched Libby's mind work. She could see her rearranging the facts of that day long ago to fit this new information. There was always more than one perspective. That's what you learn in this many decades. There were the two sides of that door, the woman in the driveway and another woman running for her life with a black eye and a scared little boy.

"I saw you all run in; I saw close the door. I saw Bruce bang on it, and I saw him out of luck."

"How did you survive?"

"Well, like I said, it came close, but it skipped this road, skipped up into the sky, and landed again, downtown, over at St. Joe's. It caused destruction at one house, and then next door, nothing. You know, we don't have hurricanes in our skies, sharks, or salt in our waters, but that tornado, and well, all of February, those are the downsides of Michigan lake life."

"Yeah, downsides," J.J. muttered.

"Aunt Emma, no one saw Bruce again," Libby pressed. "He was swept away. That's what we thought."

"No, no, he was paid off. Swept out of the way, yes, but not swept away."

"Paid off?" J.J. gasped.

"Yep, I gave him that old car I was sitting in and five thousand dollars never to come back. I was going to shoot him myself if he hurt Jackie or you or your sweet baby brother."

"Oh, my gosh, all this time, we thought..." Libby put her hands in her head, and Emma felt more than a twinge of guilt now. Her niece was a good-hearted person, and this had weighed on her, Emma saw now.

"Well, I didn't really know the internal workings of the fevered mind of a seventeen-year-old girl. I did hear you all whisper, but well, I kept my mouth shut. Hoped the man would stay gone. And he has."

"So, he didn't die in the tornado. He's alive," J.J. said.

"I wouldn't go so far as to say he's alive. I mean, he had a pretty strong cocaine habit, a bad temper, and that car I gave him had iffy steering. He could have died, by now, but he didn't die in that twister. I got rid of him for you girls though."

The two women sat there, looking at Emma. It was a look she got, now and again. She spoke her mind and always did, but somehow now, in the body of a sweet old lady, it caused jaws to drop. Back in her day, it would get her grounded, or a new boyfriend, or out of a speeding ticket, but today, well, it was shocking apparently.

"So that threat you made, to call the media or the police?" Libby ventured.

"Just me playing hardball and guessing right that you thought you did worse than you did. That's one of your fatal flaws, my dear, you never do anything all that bad, but you always torture yourself," Emma said.

"Oh, totally true," J.J. agreed instantly. "She never forgave herself for kissing Henry while dating Keith, like it was a breach of the Treaty of Versailles instead of a high school girl doing a little research on who was a better kisser."

J.J. and Emma laughed together over Libby's proclivity to think the worst of her missteps. Everyone made missteps.

"So, are we all set then? I need to get Patrick to bring the car around if we're all set."

"We're all set."

"Girls, I'm very proud of you. You stood up to Bruce back then, and you stood up to the mayor now. And I am sorry I let you think the worst. I am. But, well, I was a bit desperate myself. I've lived here my whole life, and it's quite special. It needs some love. It needs you two to cheerlead for it like you just did. But it doesn't need some fancy pants company coming in and tearing it all down."

"True that," J.J. said.

"Am I forgiven?"

Emma didn't want her niece to be cross with her. She was at the stage of life where she knew each day was a gift, and you never let 'I love you' go unsaid.

But she was also, as the kids say today, out of foxes to give if someone didn't like her methods. Her methods worked. Spectacularly so, this time!

"Yes, you're forgiven. Sort of," Libby mumbled.

"Okay, well then, I'm sort of sorry, but the person who you really need to forgive is yourself. That man was a menace, and you stood up for your friend. I say that is something to be proud of, not stew over for one more minute."

Emma stood up and put her pocketbook on her wrist.

She'd let the girls hash this out, relive the moment, make peace with the past, whatever they needed to do.

She'd done what was required, and now, she really needed to take a nap.

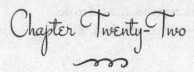

Chapter Twenty-Two

Libby

Libby had the food set out, the wine decanted, beer in the cooler, and enough snacks to feed an army. Somehow, in her short time back here, she'd amassed enough friends to require Costco quantities of potato chips.

J.J. and Dean were coming. So were Jared, Shelly, Ned, and Keith.

She hoped Keith would bring his two sons who lived in town so she could formally meet them. Arrow Orwig wanted to come, but he was working, so he arranged for bags of ice to show up at her door! She'd need it, it was going to border on hot today.

It was all too much, too sweet, so quickly.

And the weather was perfect. It was shaping up to be a great way to start the lake season.

Each morning as Libby enjoyed her coffee on the back deck, new boats, new friendly hello waves greeted her as she prepared for her day.

People loved this lake. Some lived here all summer, some

booked the same week every July, and some, like her party guests, lived here year-round.

It was a beautiful place. She hoped she could do the things it needed. She hoped her aunt's faith was well placed.

Aunt Emma was something else. Libby was still trying to process what her aunt had said. That Bruce wasn't harmed in the slightest by the tornado.

Still, it was hard to shake the feeling that she'd be able to close the door on another human. But J.J. had helped her with some of that guilt.

"You've got two daughters. What would you have told them to do? Let the wolf in the house or close the door?"

In that light, it wasn't a hard question.

"I would have said close it, lock it, and run for the cellar."

"Right, which is what you did, and I'm grateful, even more grateful now, knowing that we won't burn in hell for it."

"Right."

It would take a while to change her thinking. It was like losing weight. You still felt the heaviness at certain times, even though it was gone.

You get used to carrying baggage even after you've checked it.

Libby had a full plate of things to do for Irish Hills and not a lot of time to do them. Six months wasn't a lot of time.

But she did feel lighter. She had a lot to worry about if she wanted to make the most of her presentation to the council. But she also didn't want to sink back into a life where work pushed away moments like this. She wanted a life with plenty of room to celebrate the little miracles of every day and the big victory they'd just enjoyed. Was that within reach?

Her phone buzzed. She didn't recognize the number, but she was a mother. She always picked up. What if it was the kids?

"Libby Mal—Quinn, Libby Quinn speaking." Libby was working hard to get used to using her name, not Henry's.

"Ms. Quinn! So glad we got a hold of you before the weekend."

"That you did. What can I do for you?"

"This is Warren Bateman in New York. I require a CEO and have been looking high and low. I recently saw what you're doing in Irish Hills, what you've done for the Southtown neighborhood, and want to try to woo you here."

"Excuse me?" Libby had heard of Warren Bateman. Everyone had.

"Sorry, I realize this is out of the blue. But my foundation has a project that would be similar to what you did in Chicago, but times about ten."

"Well, I'm really not in the market for a new position."

"I know you left Chicago; can you give us a chance to show you what we're aiming for here? The funding for this is, let's just say, significant. It is a chance to make an impact beyond one neighborhood."

"Uh, well, what do you have in mind?" Libby had no clue where this was coming from. But she also wasn't stupid; when one of the richest men in the country called, you listened.

"We'd love to fly you in, show you our offices, lay out all the resources that you'd be able to harness, and just well, let you get to know us here."

"Okay, why don't you email me details? I'm really underwater right now with a project but, maybe." Never answer one way or another right away. Reginald Bellamy had taught her that one. It gave you a chance to think. Even if the answer was yes, don't jump at it.

"Wonderful, no pressure—well, some pressure. We're willing to do anything we can to make this your dream scenario."

Libby hung up the phone and, for a moment, was stunned. What in the world? A few weeks ago, she couldn't get arrested after nearly getting arrested. And now, a plum had fallen into her lap.

Well, she'd check out her email later. It was time to live in the present, thanks to the dozen people she'd invited over. No matter what tomorrow had in store, today, they were going to kick off lake season in style.

"Okay, do you remember that time you were swimming across the lake, and Trevor the Killer Swan was after you?" J.J. said as she walked out to the back porch.

Libby's guests were gathered in little packs, but all outside. J.J., Keith, Dean, and Keith's son Braylon were on the back porch. Keith's other son was out on the dock. There was a helpful crew trying to see if her pontoon boat was a lost cause. Nice of them, really. She hadn't had time to try to take it out.

"Wait, Trevor the Killer Swan?"

Bless his heart, Braylon was interested in the old stories about his dad, the lake, and their silly adventures.

"Yeah, I mean, swans are beautiful, but you know they can be stupid mean, and Trevor was that. He just had it out for us," J.J. said.

"He really did. I was in this phase where I was determined I could swim the length of the lake and back." Libby couldn't wait to swim in the lake again. Skiing was the closest she'd gotten, and that day, she was focused on skimming the surface, not slicing through it. She couldn't imagine swimming the distances she did back in the day, and with no life jacket. She'd kill her kids if they tried it.

"So, Libby is halfway out, and your dad and the rest of us are on the raft. All of a sudden, Trevor the Killer Swan decides he's Jaws. Libby is out there, swimming as fast as she can, and Trevor is honking his evil swan lungs out at her."

"He was between me and the raft, and coming in hot, as they say," Libby said.

"What was he going to do?" Braylon said.

"I don't know. Peck at me with his beak? Smack me with his wings? I couldn't tell you what the actual threat was, but it was a threat. That's all I know. I think I screamed."

183

"Oh, you screamed, 'TREVOR! Take a CHILL PILL!'" J.J. said.

"Oh, gosh, yes, quite the war cry."

"So, then your dad, who at that time was probably the best Hacky Sack player in all of Lenawee County—" J.J. said, referring to Keith.

"Probably? I was the Magic Johnson of Hacky Sack at that time," Keith said.

Libby laughed out loud, a laugh that was not ladylike, a real honking laugh.

"That's a GREAT impression of the sound Trevor was making," Keith quipped.

Libby wanted to tell Keith not to tease her, but she could barely catch her breath.

J.J. continued the epic tale. "Okay, so our hero here stands up on the raft, squares up like a superhero or something, and yells that he's got it. He whips that Hacky Sack as hard as he can. Really rifles it out there and HITS Trevor in the wing."

"It was Tom Brady level accuracy, trust me," Keith said to Braylon, who could not have rolled his eyes any higher in their sockets.

"Trevor honked in protest, and if that bird could have flipped us the bird with his feathers, he would have. So, Trevor stands down, and Keith waves Libby in, you know, all clear from attack swans," J.J. said.

"Peak heroics," Keith said.

Libby was crying. She was laughing so hard.

She'd forgotten that moment.

How had she forgotten?

She was just so grateful to be here, with people who reminded her.

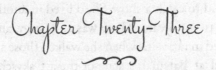

Chapter Twenty-Three

Libby

It took Libby longer to drive to the airport than to fly to New York.

The flight from Detroit Metro to LaGuardia was a quick two hours, and it was first class.

When Warren Bateman offered to pick her up, fly her first class, and threw in a ticket to a Broadway show, saying no seemed almost rude.

Her trip was going to be one quick overnight. A whirlwind, really. She didn't tell anyone. It was amazing to her that she had people to tell.

Her aunt, J.J., and even Keith were now fixtures in her life. They would care if she was gone, where she went, if she was okay.

Libby didn't know why she didn't tell anyone. Anyway, she'd be there and back before anyone knew she was gone.

She had donned her lone power suit again. There was a time when she had every shade of black, gray, and tan. There was a time when she loved her stilettoes. She'd gotten rid of all of it but for this one ensemble. Was that some sort of sign that she wasn't ready to leave it all behind?

There was a car waiting for her at the airport. Her driver took her into the city. She'd been to NYC over the years for shopping, conferences, and to catch a show. She'd lived in another major city for more than twenty years. There was an energy, an electricity to it, that hummed in her veins when she walked those sidewalks.

She arrived at Bateman's state-of-the-art skyscraper and was greeted by a woman whose suit was probably three times as expensive as Libby's.

"How was your trip?"

"Smooth as silk, thank you."

The woman led Libby to a bank of elevators. Libby had a long stride. She was used to walking in heels, but they pinched for some reason as the spikes hit the marble floor.

Libby's ears popped as the elevator sped up to the top floor of the Bateman Building.

They made their way to a reception area and into the top floor office. Libby tried to play it cool, but it was impossible. The billion-dollar view of Manhattan that filled her vision was unbelievable.

"Wow, stunning," she said.

"Thank you, yes, I'm Warren. I am here every day and never get over it either." The voice came from behind her. Libby whipped her head around to see Warren Bateman, one of the riches men in the world, gaze at his own view.

Warren Bateman was a billionaire. He had inherited a fortune and had parlayed that into billions more. But in the last few years, he'd been making headlines for his philanthropic projects and gifts.

Libby deduced that was how she'd landed on his radar. She was —*was* being the operative word—on an upward trajectory of community development.

"Yes, so glad to meet you but—" Libby didn't want to be rude.

Warren Bateman had foot the bill for terrific accommodations. It was time to hear just what he had in mind for her.

"Why are you here? Yes, well, one of my greatest joys in the last few years is the Global Home Fund. With it, we've built hospitals, funded research, and fought injustice, so many things that are important to the world."

Libby was aware, and it was impressive. "I know the GHF has made a big impact in a wide range of causes."

"Yes, and my newest, will be exactly up your ally, right in the wheelhouse of your expertise. I am starting the Global Home Neighborhood Project. There will be billions in funding. We plan to select worthy projects and find places in the deepest need and fund those needs."

"How would I fit in with that?"

"Oh, at the very top. I'd lean on you to create a vetting process, hire directors, really manage it from here."

"Most of my experience is at the grassroots level." Libby would be lying, though, if she didn't say she was flabbergasted and amazed that this billionaire philanthropist was interested in her for such a plum position.

"Your recent victory was in, in ah—small-town Michigan? I read the news article."

"Well, that's a work in progress."

"I understand where you're coming from, but you're ready to be at a higher level. That doesn't mean you'll do less good. It means more. You'll have access to all our resources. In fact, my assistant, whom you met, will show you your suite of offices in this very building. I am committed to the project and hear you're the woman who can make sure we get this done."

"Thank you."

Warren Bateman outlined her role, his visions. He talked about her being an ambassador in the media and in communities for his projects.

It was a dream job. But it was more than that. It was overwhelming to hear about. It seemed impossible.

But in many ways, it was the opposite of what she liked best. Libby always saw her place in the neighborhoods as finding the smallest issues and working one project at a time.

After making his pitch, the Bateman's assistant appeared again, as if from thin air.

"Your next meeting is here."

"Yes, yes. I have to go, but I need an answer. I am not a person who waits, one of my few flaws. I'm going to go head to my conference room. Make yourself at home here, have a think on what you require to make this deal, and I'll be back soon to button it up."

Warren Bateman said it with confidence. There was no doubt in his mind that she would jump at the opportunity.

And it was an amazing opportunity. One that she'd have clawed to get only a year ago, heck, maybe even a month ago.

Libby looked around the spacious office. Her gaze was pulled out toward the city, to the streets. She was being offered the chance to help from up here.

Libby walked along the curved wall of the office. There were pictures of Warren Bateman with Nobel Prize winners, presidents, and tycoons.

Then one photo stopped her in her tracks.

It was Warren Bateman and Bill Gates, but something about it was familiar.

She studied it again, all thoughts of the offer pushed aside. Where was this? Why had she seen it? And then it hit her.

The picture had been taken at Stirling Resorts Las Vegas Grand. She had seen it as she researched for her presentation to the Irish Hills council!

"Wait a minute." This time she actually said it out loud.

Warren Bateman had congratulated her for her work in Irish Hills.

This had only just happened. Irish Hills didn't have a daily paper. No news outlet had even looked twice at the goings-on in Irish Hills. There was no way Bateman could have known what she'd done to delay eminent domain, from several states away in his skyscraper. There had been zero coverage of it.

Unless.

Libby walked out to the receptionist.

"Can you tell Mr. Bateman that I'm going to have to run? I have another appointment."

This might be a good offer, but Warren Bateman had not been watching her. He didn't give two cents about her career or skills.

She knew it without a doubt.

Libby was a pawn on Stone Stirling's chessboard, and he wanted her moved. If he couldn't beat her at city council meetings, he'd remove her this way.

Stone Stirling had found a way to get rid of her, by finding her another job. It was an amazing job, and by arranging this opportunity, he could remove her from the fight in Irish Hills.

Well, too darn bad, billionaires. Too darn bad.

Libby checked into her hotel room. She may as well have a good night! But it was going to be on her own terms. She would not be wearing these god-awful heels again unless it was a life-or-death situation.

And the Spanx had to go. Libby hung up her power suit, hopefully for good, and then she hooked her fingers into the waistband of her Spanx. She pulled, shimmied, lost her balance, and fell onto the bed.

Getting out of a pair of Spanx was like being born again, but not in a good way, though she did pray to God at one point.

She tossed the shapewear and fished out her leggings and cute tennis shoes. She'd go see a show, walk around the city, and think. But her thoughts weren't about this big job in New York. No, her thoughts were about Irish Hills and how to fulfill the promises she'd made.

* * *

Within twenty-four hours, she was back at Nora House. Her power suit was back in the closet, ready for the next dance with the city council, but retired from interviewing, she decided.

This was her home, for now.

She felt lighter, happier, but at the same time filled with purpose.

A familiar sound alerted Libby that she had a visitor, but one who didn't use the driveway but the dock.

Keith.

She felt a flutter in her stomach, at the sight of him, on his boat. She went out back and helped make sure the boat put in softly without a scratch to the glossy wood finish of his vintage Chris-Craft.

She tied the front rope to the front; he did the same with the back.

"To what do I owe this visit?"

"I was worried."

"What?"

"I was worried. I came by yesterday, and no you."

"Oh, yeah, sorry about that. I had to go out of town really quick."

"And you didn't tell me, or your aunt, or J.J? I was ready to call the Lenawee County Sheriff's Office."

"I didn't think anyone would notice," Libby lied. She had thought that maybe they would. She didn't want to tell them what she had considered. It felt like a betrayal after how hard they'd all worked, after they'd all embraced her and trusted her without missing a beat. Even though they'd missed decades together.

"Of course we noticed. I noticed."

They were on the dock. Waves lapped quietly on the boat, and the sun was rising in the sky heading toward noon.

The air shifted between them. The thing he'd said was maybe meant from friend to friend but landed differently.

He'd noticed she was gone.

Libby swallowed hard. Keith took a breath. And then he put his hand on Libby's cheek. She drew close, and their lips met. It was as before. There was a spark, an extra sizzle when they were this close, something Libby hadn't felt with any other person.

Keith stepped back.

"Wow, K," Libby said. "You're still a darn good kisser, though the gray stubble is new."

"Yeah? Well, same to you."

Libby laughed. Tears escaped from the corner of her eyes. Good tears from how good this new chapter of her life was. Familiar in some ways but also brand new. She wasn't expecting to find purpose or friendships and had never once thought about dating.

"I ought to push you off the dock for that," Libby said.

"If I'm going down, you're coming with me, Q."

They held hands for a moment and didn't say anything else. Libby didn't know what was next for them. She hoped it was another kiss. But she didn't plan any further than that. She'd let it play out however it was supposed to. Her life had been filled with detailed plans. With Keith, at least for now, she was going to let things happen as they were meant to, or not.

"Well, now that I know you're alive, I'm going to check on your pontoon. J.J. expects a level of comfort out here that you're not going to live up to if you do not have a workable pontoon."

"Yes, sir. Can I get you anything? Do we even have tools here? I have no idea."

"The tools I need are all in the boat, but you know a cold drink is always appreciated."

"Coming right up."

Keith squeezed her hand, they locked eyes again, and Libby felt safe, happy. There was a person here, who could very well be the next big thing in her life, but she wasn't in a hurry for the first time in a long time.

"Lemonade sound good?"

"Sounds perfect."

The plan had been to hide out here until she figured out what was next. This place was next. She needed to be in Irish Hills, and it turned out Irish Hills needed her.

As Libby headed back to the house to get the refreshments, her phone buzzed from her back pocket.

She glanced at it and recognized the number. It was from a Manhattan area code.

Libby ignored it.

Chapter Twenty-Four

Libby

Aunt Emma insisted on going with her. The idea that she'd be in a Detroit Pawnshop with her ninety-year-old aunt, hocking her wedding ring, and her aunt's diamond necklace, was ludicrous.

But here they were.

"Do you know Rick?"

Aunt Emma thought that all pawnshop owners knew each other, apparently. She was sure that the owners of Detroit Pawnshop knew the Pawn Stars guys.

"Aunt Emma, Rick's pawnshop is on a TV show. They're in Las Vegas, for goodness' sake."

The man behind the counter smiled. "Actually, I met him at a convention. He was the speaker."

Aunt Emma shot Libby a look of victory. This was proof that all pawnshop owners knew each other.

"The value here, between the ring and the necklace, will be enough," Aunt Emma said confidently. Aunt Emma said most things confidently, Libby noticed.

Libby needed cash to pay roofers for the downtown buildings, now.

The grant application was on track but not fast enough. They needed a roof immediately, or the damage inside from weather would triple the project's cost.

Libby planned to pawn her wedding ring, and her aunt got wind of it and insisted that her necklace was worth three times Libby's ring.

Again, Aunt Emma was right. The necklace was stunning. Libby felt zero worry about pawning her own ring, but pawning Emma's jewelry had her nervous.

"Don't worry, this nice man will keep it safe, we'll get the money we need, and then we'll come on back when we can repay him."

"You'll have forty-five days, fewer fees, services charges, and interest rates, of course."

"Of course," said Libby.

"It's not life or death, it's baubles, and they're doing more good here than around our necks and fingers."

Aunt Emma was right. Still, she'd dragged her old aunt to a pawn shop. Though her old aunt loved every minute of it.

They had the money to pay to start the roof. Libby hoped that soon, they'd have the money for the entire project, or she'd be investigating selling organs.

If she had to, she'd take out a mortgage on Nora House for the money to fund the downtown project. She hoped it wouldn't come to that. Libby liked to be as debt-free as she could be. But if push came to shove, that was the next option.

A few days after her pawnshop adventure, Libby and J.J. sat on the porch at Nora House. After a long day of deciding things like roof tile, gutter materials, and light fixtures, it felt good to unwind.

She and J.J. brainstormed most nights. There were a million decisions to make. J.J. was the perfect foil for Libby's worry about every little detail. In other words, J.J. brought wine.

Libby was opening email on her phone while sipping a red from a place called Cherry Creek. It was good, but she nearly spit it out when the other shoe dropped in the form of the latest email from the grant committee liaison.

"We have to figure out exactly what we want downtown," Libby said to J.J., reading the email.

"Okay, we can do that, no problem. I'd like a chocolatier."

"Well, yes, but here's the problem, we need commitments from tenants. The committee needs an actual plan for each space. To get all the funding, the grant committee wants to see that we're offering something important to Irish Hills. Exactly what we're offering, with detailed business commitments."

"So, a vape shop and an edible underwear boutique won't cut it?" J.J. was trying to keep Libby from spinning out.

"Ha, ha. This is serious. We literally must come up with a definitive business plan for the establishments we are planning to attract. And we have to do it fast. This is our competition."

Libby slid her phone to J.J.

J.J.'s eyes got wide. "This looks great. Where is it? Let's move there!"

Their competition for the grant funds had commitments from a restaurant chain, a fitness studio, and a children's clothing shop. Libby had commitments from exactly no one. There was no guarantee that once the space was ready, anyone would want to rent it.

"See? Right. They get the money, or we do." Libby's heart rate increased. She felt like she was in a sprint.

"Okay, okay, so what do we think goes in this space? What does downtown Irish Hills need, what do summer visitors want?"

"I think we for sure need a gift shop, every lake town has one, and the gas station isn't cutting it when it comes to gifts. Or maybe a clothing boutique or home décor? For sure, a restaurant. Or a pizza place? Maybe a bookstore?"

"Oh, so everything but the kitchen sink," J.J. said.

"Yes, and we can't just wish for it. We must have agreements with businesses that they're coming. That they're willing to open up shop."

"Do you know anyone willing to open a restaurant in Irish Hills in its current state?" J.J. asked.

"No. That is our catch-22. No one wants to open a business here because it is falling apart, but we need to entice a business to come here to fix it. And I am fresh out of favors after getting the gas station contract for Arrow."

"I know someone."

They turned to find Aunt Emma walking onto the porch. She used her hand on the porch rail to support her steps, but she was there. And she had an unmistakable twinkle in her eyes.

"She's like Beetlejuice. Did you say her name three times or something?" J.J. said under her breath.

"Shh." Libby laughed in spite of herself.

"Who do you know? And how did you get here? Patrick?"

"Yes, I told him to wait in the car. I won't be long."

"What are you up to?"

"Oh, I know of someone who would be perfectly suited to open an eatery in Irish Hills."

"Who?"

Aunt Emma produced a neatly folded newspaper clipping. She handed it to Libby. The clip was from *The Cincinnati Enquirer*.

Libby opened it and staring back at her was a picture of a pretty woman holding a casserole toward the camera.

Libby read the article out loud.

Covington Woman Wins Third Consecutive Cincinnati's Best Dishes Title

"Marcia H. Venerable has done it again. This year her Crustless Zucchini Pie takes the cake! The judges' comments ranged from 'delicious' to 'over the top'! Venerable garnered high marks for her use of seasonal ingredients, local cheeses, and her presentation. One judge exclaimed that the entry was 'crack in a casserole dish.' This is Venerable's third consecutive title at the Best Dishes competition. Her win qualifies the chef for a spot on the USA Best Dishes event in Las Vegas. Venerable runs Venerable Catering out of her Covington home."

Libby looked at the photo. What caught her eye first was the woman's hair. It was long and piled on top of her head. Two snowy white streaks, chunks really, escaped in the front and framed her face. The chef smiled at the camera and held a blue ribbon and her award-winning dish in her hands.

"She's beautiful. I am jealous of that hair," J.J. said.

"She is," said Libby. But she also saw fatigue, even a little frenzy, in the image. Libby imagined a baking competition was a high-stress situation.

"So, why do you have this article?" Libby asked Aunt Emma.

"Look again. She's the solution to your conundrum about a restaurant in downtown Irish Hills."

Libby and J.J. refocused on the photo.

"Oh my gosh!" J.J. gasped.

And it dawned on Libby at the exact same time.

"That's Hope!" Libby exclaimed.

"Yes, another of your Sandbar Sisters. Go get her!" Aunt Emma clapped her hands as though the woman in the photo would magically appear.

Could it be true, could Libby and J.J. bring Hope back to Irish Hills? And would she be open to the idea of jumping into the whirlwind resuscitating the downtown?

Libby had no idea what had happened in Hope's life since they'd last seen her. But if she'd learned anything in the last few weeks, it was that she'd made a mistake in her own life by losing touch with her Sandbar Sisters.

Maybe, this was the right time to reconnect with Hope. Maybe Hope was the right person for the new era of Irish Hills.

Libby was game to find out.

"Okay, I'll give it a try," Libby said.

"Oh good. It's settled then." Aunt Emma waved her hand and left them on the porch.

In Aunt Emma's mind, it was settled. Libby knew a million things could go sideways with all their plans.

"To the Sandbar Sisters," J. J. said and lifted her wine glass.

"To the Sandbar Sisters," Libby echoed and lifted her glass as well.

The two women clinked glasses, and Libby imagined a future where another glass might join the toast and turn their duo into a trio.

The Sandbar Sisters Story Continues in the next book of The Summer Cottage Novels. Check out Sandbar Season.

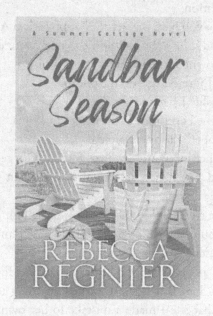

About the Author

Rebecca Regnier is an award-winning newspaper columnist and former television news anchor. She lives in Michigan with her family and handsome dog. For all the latest from the beach sign up for her newsletter by visiting BeachyReads.com. Or follow her on one of her socials. She loves share laughs with her readers!

- tiktok.com/@rebeccaregnier
- facebook.com/rlregnier
- instagram.com/rebeccaregnier
- bookbub.com/authors/rebecca-regnier

Also by Rebecca Regnier

Summer Cottage Novels

- Sandbar Sisters
- Sandbar Season
- Sandbar Summer
- Sandbar Storm
- Sandbar Sunset

Widow's Bay Paranormal Women's Fiction Mysteries

North of Forty-Nine Paranormal Women's Fiction Adventure

Kendra Dillon Suspense Thrillers (As Rebecca Rane)